I0770774

The
Wasted
Pawn

a 509 Crime Story

by Colin Conway

The Wasted Pawn

Cover Design by Rob Williams

ISBN: 978-1-961030-36-7

Original Ink Press, an imprint of High Speed Creative, LLC
1521 N. Argonne Road, #C-205
Spokane Valley, WA 99212

Visit the author's website at colinconway.com

What is the 509?

Separated by the Cascade Range, Washington State is divided into two distinctly different climates and cultures.

The western side of the Cascades is home to Seattle, its 34 inches of annual rainfall, and the incredibly weird and smelly Gum Wall. Most of the state's wealth and political power are concentrated in and around this enormous city. The residents of this area know the prosperity that has come from being the home of Microsoft, Amazon, Boeing, and Starbucks.

To the east of the Cascade Mountains lies nearly two-thirds of the entire state, a lot of which is used for agriculture. Washington State leads the nation in producing apples, it is the second-largest potato grower, and it's the fourth for providing wheat.

This eastern part of the state can enjoy more than 170 days of sunshine each year, which is important when there are more than 200 lakes nearby. However, the beautiful summers are offset by harsh winters, with average snowfall reaching 47 inches and the average high hovering around 37°.

While five telephone area codes provide service to the westside, only 509 covers everything east of the Cascades, a staggering twenty-one counties.

Of these, Spokane County is the largest with an estimated population of 506,000.

And, after all, what is a lie?
'tis but the truth in a masquerade.

- Lord Byron

The
Wasted
Pawn

a 509 Crime Story

1

The Unforgiving Sun

Rodney McCready dragged a twisted aluminum screen door from the barn. He threw it onto a knee-high pile of debris. He'd cleaned junk from this dilapidated structure for the past hour, but he still didn't see the point of the effort. Rodney could remove all the garbage from inside the barn and it still wouldn't be usable. The sagging roof had holes in it, and there were missing boards along the walls. The dirt floor wasn't even level. To make matters worse, the whole thing reeked of cat urine.

At first, Rodney thought there once might have been a meth lab in the barn. Now, he believed the outbuilding was a home for feral cats. That seemed worse to Rodney than being around corrosive chemicals. It meant he'd been working all morning inside a large cat box. The easiest option would be to burn the structure to the ground—contents and all. Nothing about the damn barn was worth saving.

AC/DC's "Highway to Hell" pumped through an old boom box near the barn doors.

Across a dirt driveway stood a dingy white house. Gray shingles curled and popped from the roof. Empty beer bottles lined the porch railing. Three flags hung in the front windows—the American, the Confederate, and the Gadsden. The yellow *Dont Tread on Me* flag was a historically correct representation of the banner designed by Brigadier General Christopher Gadsden, including the missing apostrophe. Rodney had learned the flag's history shortly after arriving at the Farm.

Several dusty pickups clustered in front of the garage. One of them belonged to Rodney. The others were owned by the Family. A single black Lexus had arrived while Rodney was inside the barn. He hadn't heard it pull up. Rodney also missed seeing its occupant exit.

He stepped further away from the debris pile for a better look at the car. The sedan and its shiny exterior looked out of place for this part of the state.

"You done?"

Wiley Jones slouched on an aluminum lawn chair in the shade of a willow tree. He was a small man in his early thirties. A straw cowboy hat covered his long, greasy hair. He wore a faded black Metallica T-shirt, dirty blue jeans, and unlaced combat boots. Wiley sipped iced tea from a plastic tumbler. A pitcher of the concoction sat on a small round table. Next to the jug lay a revolver.

The afternoon sun beat down on the Farm. Rodney didn't know what the day's temperature might reach because he couldn't check his cell phone. The Old Man forbade Rodney from having one while at the Farm. The other members of the Family could carry their devices, but they'd been around longer and had already proven their loyalty. He didn't even dare bring his phone in his truck, so he left it in his apartment.

Rodney wiped the sweat from his brow with his forearm. His T-shirt clung wetly to him, and he pulled it away from his chest. Nothing helped cool him down.

Wiley shifted forward in his seat, the metal squeaking as he moved. "You hear what I asked?"

"What's that?" Rodney cupped a hand to his ear and pretended not to understand the man over the crunchy guitars coming from the boom box.

"Why you stopping?"

Rodney shrugged. "I'm thirsty."

"Too bad." Wiley slumped back in his chair and languidly sipped his drink. "You ain't earned a break."

"You got plenty to share."

"It's not for you." Wiley lifted his chin toward the barn. "Get back inside."

Rodney stepped toward the house. "I'll drink from the garden hose."

"No, you won't." Wiley put his free hand on the gun.

Rodney stopped walking. "You'll shoot me if I get some water?"

"I'll shoot you if you go near the house."

"I'm dehydrated."

"Swallow your spit."

Rodney frowned. "You want me passing out?"

"It'll get the same result."

"Which is what?"

Wiley motioned the gun toward the outbuilding. "Less talk. More hustle."

Rodney started back inside the barn when there was a break in the music. That's when the screen door to the house popped open. Rodney stopped and looked back.

A man in a suit stood in the open doorway. He was tall with broad shoulders, and his dark hair was cut in a businessman's style. The guy looked as if he could have stepped off the cover of *GQ* magazine.

The next song blared through the boom box.

"Stop eye-fucking the house," Wiley ordered. He stalked toward Rodney now with his iced tea in one hand and the gun in the other. "Get in the goddamn barn!"

Rodney held up his hands in surrender. "Shoot a man

for getting heatstroke."

He walked toward the back of the barn with thoughts of the Lexus racing through his mind. How long had it been there? Did Rodney not notice it on the previous times he'd taken trash out to the debris pile? Or had the car's owner only arrived for a quick visit?

Rodney grabbed a couple of dining room chairs and carried them into the sunlight. He tossed them onto the debris pile.

A dusty haze floated along the driveway after the departing Lexus. The house lay about a hundred yards away from the roadway. The car turned onto Highway 155 and sped north to Omak.

Wiley waved his gun at the barn's opening. "I'm not telling you again."

"Yeah, yeah," Rodney mumbled.

He entered the barn once more. Rodney hated the demeaning work, but the heat made him extra irritable. The day's dry air felt like sandpaper in his lungs. He thought about taking his time, but the overriding smell of cat piss discouraged that.

Rodney found a pair of swim flippers and an old dive tank with its air supply hoses still attached. Why did anyone need diving equipment on the Farm? Rodney grabbed those items and headed toward the barn's opening. The music stopped before he reached the sunlight.

"Wiley says you need a drink."

Saxon Peckham stood near the boom box. The Old Man had an enormous head with large, expressive eyes. His teeth seemed too big for his mouth. As a result, his jaw usually hung open. When Saxon closed his lips, it looked as if he were struggling to contain his words. He wore faded denim overalls with a grimy white T-shirt underneath. His work boots were scuffed and sandy.

Rodney tossed the flippers and dive tank onto the debris pile. "It's hot as hell today."

"You weren't trying to spy our guest?"

"Hell no. I wasn't spying." Rodney flicked his thumb toward the barn. "It smells like piss in there. If you didn't want me seeing who was here, I would have stood around back. Or I could have stayed home."

Saxon's eyes narrowed. "I wanted you to clean out the barn." The Old Man stepped closer and loomed over Rodney. "Everybody has a role to serve. You think you're better than the rest of us?"

Rodney inhaled deeply. "No, sir." The dry air grated against his lungs.

Saxon nodded twice, then he turned to consider the debris pile. "You made a good dent."

"I tried."

"Wiley says you were dogging it."

Rodney looked at the other man. Wiley smirked, challenging him to do something.

"What do you say to that?" Saxon asked.

"Not much I can say." Rodney knew better than to make excuses, especially since his place in the pecking order was tenuous. "I guess I better work harder."

"That so?" the Old Man asked.

"Yes, sir."

Saxon peered into the barn, then he glanced up at the sun. "Still need that drink?"

Rodney nodded. "Please."

"All right." Saxon waved at the debris pile. "Put that shit back where you found it, then get yourself some water." The Old Man started for the house.

"Put it back?"

Saxon stopped to study Rodney. "Problem?"

"I hauled all that crap out like you asked."

"Now I'm telling you to put it back." Saxon cocked his head. "What aren't you understanding?"

It was busy work. Something to keep Rodney occupied and away from the house while the guests were inside.

"I understand," he said.

"Well, don't look so proud about it." Saxon headed toward the house. "If you make quick work of it," he said over his shoulder, "I might give you a job."

***

Rodney tossed the air tank and swim fins onto the original pile of trash. It was his fourth trip back inside the barn. Even though he had to breathe in the aroma of cat urine, he lingered in the darkness. He desperately needed a drink of water. His lips felt chapped, and his throat and lungs burned. If he wanted, he could probably say screw the whole mess.

Unfortunately, he'd have to go inside the house for his truck keys. Saxon made Rodney hang them on a wall hook whenever he arrived at the Farm. It was one more way the Old Man controlled Rodney's life whenever they were together.

Who knew what Saxon would do if Rodney wanted to leave now? Rodney didn't want to find out. He'd put in too much effort to quit.

The AC/DC music stopped again.

Rodney glanced over his shoulder at the barn's opening. No one was there, but Rodney figured it was time to go. If the cassette ended, Wiley would leave his chair to flip it over. Rodney didn't want the other man to see him lollygagging. He shuffled toward the sunlight.

Outside, Wiley crouched near the boom box. He held two cassette cases in his hand. "Pick up the pace."

"I'm trying."

"Dragging ass won't impress the Old Man." Wiley stabbed the Eject button and the cassette door popped open.

"Me dying of dehydration won't impress him, either."

Wiley chuckled. "How do you know?" He pulled out the AC/DC cassette and slipped it into a plastic case. "Maybe it'll show Saxon how far you'll go for the Family."

Rodney grabbed a rusted bicycle frame from the pile and slung it over his shoulder. Then he picked up two bald car tires. "If I die, what'll he do with my body?"

"What do you think?"

"Toss me on the heap?"

Wiley paused before slipping the second cassette into the boom box. "No, idiot. He'd call the police. The Old Man wouldn't want any trouble with the law. You having a weak constitution isn't a felony." He stabbed the Play button and Ozzy Osbourne's "Bark at the Moon" blasted through the speakers.

Rodney headed into the outbuilding with his next load. He tossed the tires onto the trash pile before shrugging off the bicycle frame. He immediately returned outside.

A blue and white Chevy Silverado bounced up the Farm's long driveway. Rodney smiled.

Nolan was back.

Wiley walked to his lawn chair, picked it up, and moved it to follow the shifting shade. He also relocated the table. When Wiley turned to settle into the chair, he noticed

Rodney still standing there. "Hey! Don't worry about him." He flopped into the aluminum chair. "Get back to work."

Rodney grabbed a handful of wood pieces and entered the barn with a quickened step. He tossed the items onto the pile and hurried outside.

The Chevy pulled alongside the house. Wiley didn't bother looking back. He didn't like Nolan. It wasn't hard to interpret his feelings after hearing Wiley repeatedly refer to Nolan as "the goddamn Canuck."

"Quit standing around with your dick in your hand," Wiley shouted over the music.

Rodney bent and grabbed a playfield for an old pinball machine. Some of the vibrant coloring had worn off, but a pirate's face and bumper scores were still visible. Rodney didn't know why the Old Man would need the playfield since there weren't any pinball machines in the house. Rodney hefted the unwieldy board and carried it inside the barn.

Sweat ran down Rodney's armpits, and his wet shirt clung to his back. He awkwardly tossed the playfield, and it fell short of the debris pile. Rodney didn't care, though. Perspiration dripped into his eyes. He dragged his palm over his forehead and into his sweaty hair. The dry air burned his throat.

Rodney returned to the blazing sun as Nolan hopped from his truck.

The Canadian crossed the driveway and headed toward the barn. Nolan Tremblay was a tall, lean man. Even in this heat, he wore a plaid shirt, blue jeans, and tan work boots. He had an angular, clean-shaven face. He carried a bottle of Molson beer hooked between two fingers.

"Where you going?" Wiley shouted.

Nolan didn't bother looking at the seated man. "What's it look like?"

"Leave him be."

"What're you gonna do about it, eh?"

Wiley jumped out of the folding chair but didn't move any closer. "Saxon gave him a chore."

"And you're his babysitter?" Nolan considered the last of the remaining debris pile as he approached. When he neared Rodney, he said, "You look like shit."

"Thirsty as hell."

He motioned toward the container of iced tea sitting on Wiley's table. "Go get some."

"They won't let me 'til I'm finished."

Nolan's brow furrowed. "You do something wrong?"

Rodney shook his head. "They're testing me."

"Huh." Nolan seemed to think about that. He glanced at his bottle of beer, then extended it. "Here." It was half full.

"He can't have that!" Wiley hollered over the music. He still hadn't moved away from the lawn chair.

A new song started, but Rodney didn't know its name.

"Wiley's full of shit," Nolan said. "Ignore him. Go on. Have a drink."

Rodney stared at the bottle and licked his cracking lips.

"I'm not messing with you, Rodney. Have it. Besides, it ain't doing me any good. I'm three beers into the mission, and I can't get rid of this hangover. Been two days full now. I'm gonna have to switch to some Jack and Cokes to put this banger to bed."

"I can't," Rodney said.

"You sure?"

Rodney wasn't, but he was still trying to curry favor with Saxon. The Old Man and Wiley told him he'd get something to drink after he finished. He didn't want to puss out now. He only had four, maybe five more loads to go, and he'd be done with the debris pile.

"Suit yourself," Nolan said. He turned the bottle over and poured the remaining beer out. "You see what's happening in Republic?"

Rodney watched the beer foam on the ground.

"It's crazy," Nolan continued. "I've been driving through there for years and nothing. Then some mining company says they found gold and everyone's acting like it's the second coming of Christ." Nolan tossed the beer bottle into the barn. It didn't break. "The company hasn't even started digging and people are moving there. New businesses opening left and right. That town better hope there's actually gold in them hills or people are gonna be pissed." Nolan chuckled.

"Quit standing around!" Wiley shouted. "I got better things to do than watch you two."

"Here," Nolan said. "I'll give you a hand." He reached for the pile.

"No," Rodney said. "I got it."

"More hands equals less work."

"Saxon said for me to do it."

"Suit yourself."

Rodney lifted an old car door with its window missing. He didn't know what kind of vehicle it came from. "What're you doing here? I thought you weren't coming back for another week."

"The Old Man called. Said he needed me for something."

"He tell you what it was?"

"You know I can't say." Nolan patted Rodney's shoulder. "Not until you're one of us."

"Yeah."

"Listen, we'll talk later. I need another book recommendation. That last one you gave me was pretty good." Nolan headed for the house.

"Get a move on, you!" Wiley shouted.

Rodney turned and trudged into the barn with the car door slung over his shoulder.

***

Rodney exited the barn and paused.

Wiley was gone. His lawn chair was still there, as was the small table. But the pitcher of iced tea was missing. Wiley had taken it with him. Had the guy left the pitcher behind, Rodney likely would have grabbed it and taken a healthy swig.

Rodney staggered toward the house. He bowed his head and slumped his shoulders against the unforgiving sun. Even at this late afternoon hour, it seemed the August heat never relented.

He entered the kitchen through the back door. Voices floated in from other parts of the house, but Rodney didn't bother searching for them. Instead, he grabbed a plastic tumbler from the cupboard and filled it with tap water.

Wiley's iced tea pitcher and cup sat in the sink along with several dirty plates.

Rodney drank greedily until the tumbler was empty. His gulps didn't capture all the water, and some flowed over his chin. The cool trail running down his chest felt sublime.

He refilled the tumbler but didn't guzzle the water this time. Instead, he sipped it. Rodney didn't leave the kitchen. He knew better. Only members of the Family freely moved about Saxon's home.

Rodney's gaze flicked to the wall hook where his truck keys hung. The Chevy keychain emblem faced outward. He'd been careful to place his keys that way, so he'd know if anyone had messed with them. He did that every time he visited the Farm. So far, no one had ever touched them but him.

"C'mon."

Rodney looked over his shoulder.

Kaylee Zavala stood in the doorway. The short, pale woman had recently turned twenty-four. He'd met her at the birthday party Saxon threw at the Dilly-Dally Lounge. Kaylee was anorexic thin with cruel eyes and long, stringy hair. She wore a plain red T-shirt and denim shorts, both of which looked too big for her frame. Her white Converse shoes were the only clothing properly sized.

She jerked her head toward the other room. "They're waiting."

Rodney followed without another word. They walked past a dining table into the living room. Slivers of sunlight slipped past the drawn curtains. A cigarette haze hung in the room. *Divorce Court* played on the big screen television.

Four men lounged in the room. Saxon stretched out in the large recliner with the best view of the television. A cigarette dangled between his fingers. He lowered the sound on the TV.

On the couch nearest the window, Wiley and Nolan sat at opposite ends. Each man had his feet on the coffee table. Tucker Skillingstad sprawled on the second couch with his head propped up on a pair of pillows. Every man held a bottle of Pabst.

They'd all been talking and laughing but stopped when Kaylee and Rodney entered the room. She smacked

Tucker's boots, and he lifted his feet for her to sit.

"Move your ass," Kaylee said.

"I'm comfortable."

She glared at Tucker until he swung his legs off the couch and sat upright. "Yes, Mother."

"Don't mother me."

Kaylee dropped onto the far end of the couch. Her pale complexion was in stark contrast to the men in the house. She was like a vampire, rarely exposing her skin to the sun. The men, however, had darkened extremities known as farmer tans. If they removed their shirts, their bellies were as white and soft as a fish. Rodney had seen them all down at Omak Lake a couple of weeks ago. Kaylee stayed out of the sun the entire time.

Saxon crushed his cigarette into an ashtray balanced on the recliner's armrest. His gaze cut to Rodney. "Everything put back?"

Rodney nodded, but the Old Man likely knew it was. Wiley had stayed outside until Rodney hauled the last load into the barn. That's when he carried his pitcher of iced tea inside.

"You think you're ready for a job?" Saxon asked.

"If you say so," Rodney said.

"Good answer."

Tucker winked at Rodney while Wiley glared. Nolan and Kaylee watched the nearly silent *Divorce Court*.

Rodney and Tucker had bunked together while in prison. That's where they met. It was almost a year since they both got out. Rodney reconnected with Tucker at Kaylee's recent birthday celebration. It had been a whirlwind three weeks since then. Rodney met the Family but had yet to earn Saxon's trust. Rodney heard rumors about what they did, but none of them openly talked about it in his presence. Saxon allowed Rodney to hang around the Farm like a stray dog, always putting him outside whenever there was business to discuss.

"This job," Saxon said, "you're doing it on your own. Got it? In case you fuck up."

Rodney nodded. "That way, it doesn't blow back on anyone but me. I understand. What's the job?"

Saxon shifted in his chair and leaned an elbow on the armrest. He grinned like he held a handful of aces. "You tell us."

"Yeah," Wiley chimed in. "You tell us."

The Old Man's free hand shot up. The rebuke caused Wiley to turn his attention toward the television. Nolan and Kaylee still hadn't looked away from the staged court proceedings even though they couldn't hear what the judge was saying.

Tucker watched Rodney intently. He absently drank his beer.

"You want me to find a job?" Rodney asked.

"I'm sure as hell not giving you one." Saxon kicked his bottle back and drained the remaining beer. "I don't trust you."

Wiley snickered, but his attention remained glued to the television.

"Fine," Rodney said.

Saxon tapped his empty bottle against the recliner's wooden handle. Kaylee dutifully stood and moved toward the Old Man.

Wiley watched her. "Get me another while you're at it."

Kaylee extended her middle finger. "Get it yourself." She grabbed the empty bottle from Saxon and paused next to Rodney. "Want one?"

"No, thank you."

"The hell?" Wiley said.

"Rodney doesn't demand." She disappeared into the other room.

"Two rules," Saxon said. He held up as many fingers. "You got forty-eight hours, and the split needs to net us two grand each." He motioned around the room, then thumbed toward the kitchen where Kaylee currently was.

Rodney did the math. "Ten grand?"

Saxon crinkled his nose. "You don't wanna get paid?"

"Twelve, then."

"I'd think bigger," Saxon said, "but if that's all you wanna shoot for, so be it. It's your job."

Kaylee returned to the room and handed the Old Man a beer. She brought a second one for herself.

"Thanks for nothing," Wiley muttered.

"You're welcome." She dropped into her spot on the couch and turned her attention back to the television.

"Can I bring someone in on it?" Rodney asked.

"Not from the Family, but other than that—" Saxon shrugged. "I don't care what you do, but you don't tell them you're working with us, because you aren't. This is your job. Their cut comes out of your end, not off the top. Fair?"

Rodney stared into his tumbler as he nodded.

"If you can't do it," the Old Man said, "say so now. We don't wanna waste our time with a baby bird afraid to fly."

He looked up. "I can do it."

Tucker winked at Rodney again. "What'd I tell you, Saxon? He's gonna do good."

"We'll see." The Old Man twisted the top off his beer. He flicked the cap into the dining room. "We'll see if he can spread his wings and fly." He pointed the bottle at Rodney. "Don't come back empty-handed."

"Yes, sir." Rodney backpedaled.

"All right," Saxon said. "The rest of you get out of here."

"Hot date?" Wiley asked.

The Old Man smirked. "Sometimes a man just wants to be alone without all the idiots in his life around."

Rodney spun and headed toward the back door. As he passed through the kitchen, Rodney collected his keys from the wall hook. He heard the rest of the family exit the house after him.

Outside, Wiley called after Rodney. "Baby bird, meet us at the Double D."

He looked over his shoulder. The rest of the family was filing out after Wiley.

"All right," Rodney said.

"Kaylee's gonna ride with you."

She headed Rodney's way with her hand outstretched. "I'm driving."

"Who said?"

"Me."

"It's my truck," Rodney said.

Kaylee kept her lips tight and ran her tongue around her teeth. Irritation flashed in her cruel eyes.

Rodney let the keys dangle from his fingers. "Fine. Whatever."

She snatched them and opened the driver's door. "Let's go."

2

The Suicide Shot

Kaylee drove Rodney's truck forty miles per hour along the highway, much slower than the allowed sixty. Wiley's pickup zipped around them, its horn honking wildly. Nolan passed them next. When Tucker passed them, he stuck his arm out the window and extended his middle finger above the roof.

"Why're you letting them pass us?" Rodney asked.

"Because we never get time to talk." She sat close to the steering wheel. Before leaving, they hadn't adjusted the bench seat to accommodate her size. "Tell me about yourself."

Rodney wanted to say her slow driving bothered him, but he didn't think that was what she was after. "What do you wanna know?"

"Anything. Where you're from, what you used to do, that sort of thing." Kaylee waved her hand to make it all sound innocent, but Rodney believed she was after something.

He twisted in his seat to study her. "Moses Lake," he said finally.

She cast a sideways glance. "That's where you grew up?"

"That's right."

"Still got family there?"

"No."

"How about friends?"

He shook his head. "Haven't been back since high school."

"Huh." Kaylee reached for the radio but didn't turn it on. She put her hand back on the steering wheel. "What'd you do before prison?"

"Nothing. I got arrested outside of high school."

"How many times?"

Rodney rested his arm along the back of the bench seat. "Saxon asked you to pump me for information, is that it?"

She glanced at him but quickly turned back to the road. "No." Her face pinched. "Why would you say that?"

He continued to stare at her. "Because we've never played Twenty Questions before."

"All right." She shrugged. "Maybe he did. So what? If I don't come back with some answers, he's gonna make the others ask the questions. Who would you rather interrogate you? Them or me?"

"You," he said. "Definitely." Rodney tried to make it sound like he was flirting, but the words sounded forced in his ears. He looked ahead. "Tucker already knows everything. We shared a cell. Wasn't much to talk about for all that time."

"You know how it is. The Old Man wants us to verify everything. Just to be sure."

"I get it," Rodney said, "but why are you all so secretive? I don't even know what you do out here."

The truck slowed, and Kaylee flicked on the truck's right turn blinker. "Tucker never told you?"

"He said you guys were like a waypoint."

"Like?"

Rodney shrugged. "That's what he said. He never said a waypoint for what."

Kaylee left the highway and pulled onto a dirt

driveway. A hand-painted sign sat parallel with the road. Red words once stood promptly against a white background. Now, the sun and blowing dust had worn the luster away from the marker. The words *The Dilly-Dally Lounge* took up most of the sign. Someone had added a caveat in blue spray paint. Underneath the business name, the words *By Invitation Only* were added.

Kaylee guided the pickup along the winding driveway. Up ahead stood a large, two-level house. Roughly twenty cars parked haphazardly in front of the structure.

The pickup crept along now, barely moving ten miles per hour. It bounced whenever it hit a pothole and jostled its occupants.

Rodney grabbed the dashboard to steady himself. He changed the subject since he wanted to get away from his background. "Got a boyfriend?"

Kaylee stifled a laugh as she rocked from side to side. "What?"

"Never mind." Rodney looked toward the Okanogan River. A lone kayaker paddled along the surface.

"Why would you ask that?" Kaylee asked. "You don't like me."

His flirting must have been worse than he thought.

She pulled the truck alongside Wiley's and Nolan's pickups, then turned off the engine.

Rodney scanned the other vehicles in the lot. None of them were any cleaner than Rodney's. Many had confederate flag stickers in their windows. Others had AR-15 decals or pronouncements that Rodney should fuck his feelings.

"You think I should get a sticker for my truck?" Rodney asked.

Kaylee pushed back in the seat and held out the keys.

"Don't change the subject."

"What subject?" He took the keys from her.

"I'm not your type," she said.

Rodney furrowed his brow. "How do you know?"

"I know."

"Maybe you are."

"Gimme a break," Kaylee said. "You never look at me with big eyes."

"Sure, I do."

"Whatever. I watch you." She motioned toward Wiley's and Nolan's trucks. "I watch all of you. I know who's your type."

"Who's my type?

"Electric Mary."

Rodney cocked his head. "The girl from your birthday party?"

She smirked. "Don't say it like you don't remember her."

He remembered the curvy brunette. She was like a walking wet dream.

"Nobody forgets Mary," Kaylee said. "Not even the guys who don't find her attractive."

Rodney chuckled as he spun his keys around his index finger. "She's not my type."

Kaylee barked a single laugh. "You're a terrible liar, Rodney McCready."

He prayed that wasn't true.

"Mary's your type, and she's definitely Wiley's type."

Wiley talked about Mary all the time when he wasn't yelling at Rodney. That's why Rodney didn't want anyone to know he was infatuated with the curvy brunette, too.

"What's Nolan's type?" he asked.

Kaylee jerked open the driver's door. "He likes the

Natives."

"No, shit." That's probably another reason Wiley didn't like the Canadian. "And Tucker?"

She slipped off the bench seat and turned around. "I thought you would know his type, being cellmates and all."

Rodney popped open his door. "He never said."

Tucker liked black women, but the man never spoke about it around the Family. It wasn't something a person announced openly with the way Saxon and Wiley felt about minorities.

"We had a thing once, Tucker and me." Kaylee shrugged a single shoulder. "I thought he might have told you."

Rodney shook his head. "I guess he doesn't kiss and tell."

"Huh." She slid out of the truck. "I never took him for a gentleman."

Tucker *had* told Rodney about the short-lived relationship with Kaylee. It hadn't lived up to his expectations. First, Tucker kept thinking of Kaylee as a little sister. Second, Tucker wanted to meet black women. He often took solo trips to Seattle or Spokane hoping to meet the type of women he couldn't find around a small town like Omak.

Rodney slid out of the passenger seat and closed the door. At least he proved he wasn't as bad of a liar as Kaylee thought he was.

Now, he just had to hold it together inside The Dilly-Dally.

***

A handwritten sign on the front door read *Own Your Choices. We Aren't Covering for You with Your Wife or Your Parole Officer.*

Rodney followed Kaylee inside and was immediately greeted with overly aggressive rock and roll. He liked classic rock but didn't care for the really hard stuff. An angry singer kept asking for the bodies to hit the floor. Several patrons chanted along with the song.

"Close the door," the bartender yelled.

Rodney shut it and closed off the sunlight. The bar darkened again.

The Dilly-Dally Lounge consisted of a kitchen, one large room, and a single-toilet restroom. The stairs at the far end of the room were chained off. Rodney had never been on the upper level to see what occurred there.

A bar sat against the east wall. It was smaller than those usually found in a regular establishment, but The Dilly-Dally had the feel of a private club. It wasn't, though, since it had a state approved liquor license hanging in plain view.

Neon and flashing lights hung around the main room.

There weren't any tables like a normal saloon. Instead, there were couches and soft chairs. Also, there were no pinball machines or dartboards. A large industrial fan stood in the room's corner and blew the warm air about. The air-conditioner struggled to keep up with the number of customers in the house.

Wiley, Nolan, and Tucker huddled at the bar and leered at the buxom redhead working behind it. She wore a yellow swimsuit top and denim shorts. She slid cans of Pabst in front of each guy.

The woman noticed Kaylee and Rodney. "What're you having?" she shouted.

Kaylee said, "The same."

Rodney nodded.

The bartender grabbed a couple more cans and cracked them open. She slid them in front of the newcomers.

"Let's go out back," Kaylee said. "It's hot and sticky in here." She pulled at her T-shirt.

"I thought you liked it hot and sticky," Nolan said with a leer.

"You wish."

Tucker kicked back his beer. "It's hot outside, too."

"But not as loud," Kaylee protested.

"We'll go outside in a minute," Wiley said. "Let's wink at each other first." He knocked on the counter and spun his finger.

Nolan stepped back. "Not so soon."

Tucker shook his head. "Not now."

Wiley slapped both hands onto the bar. "The fuck is wrong with you two? It's a Stampede tradition." He noticed Rodney. "And baby bird hasn't done one yet."

Rodney asked, "What are we talking about?"

Kaylee pointed at a neon writing board. Suicide Shots were listed as a special through the weekend.

"What the hell is a Suicide Shot?" Rodney asked.

Wiley flicked his hands out in an I-told-you-so manner.

Tucker rolled his eyes. "Fine. For Rodney."

Nolan lifted his beer. "For Rodney."

The bartender faced the group. "You all taking the plunge?"

Wiley nodded. "Time to initiate baby bird." He held up his hand. "Five."

Kaylee waved off the bartender. "Not me. They're not challenging my manhood again."

The bartender set four shot glasses on the counter and

poured tequila into them. Then she set a lime wedge next to each. Finally, she put the saltshaker on the counter.

Wiley looked at Rodney. "You know how to do a regular shot of tequila right? Lick the salt, drink the shot, suck the lime?"

Rodney nodded. He disliked tequila, but he'd done shots of the liquor before.

"The Suicide Shot is different," Wiley explained. "You're gonna snort the salt, drink the shot, then squeeze the lime in your eye."

Rodney looked at Tucker. "Is this for real?"

"Burns like hell," his former cellmate said.

Nolan sipped his beer and smirked at Kaylee. "This is where we separate the boys from the girls."

"You mean the smart from the stupid," she countered.

The bartender rang the brass bell at the end of the counter. "Suicide Shots!"

A callback of "No retreat! No surrender!" came from the others in the bar.

"Can't back out now," Wiley said. "Everybody's watching."

"If you're doing it—" Rodney glanced at the others. "I'm doing it."

"That's the spirit," Wiley said.

Wiley sprinkled a line of salt on the bar. He bent over and snorted it. "Ugh," he groaned and held his nose. He waited only a second before kicking back the shot of liquor. Next, Wiley grabbed the lime. He held his right eye open and squeezed the lime into it. "Shit!" he cried. Wiley covered his eye with his hand and danced around in a circle.

The bar erupted in cheers and claps. Several patrons stood to watch the ritual.

"You're up," the bartender said to Rodney.

He waved her off. "I'll wait."

"Waiting makes it worse," Kaylee said.

Nolan grabbed the saltshaker and shook out a line before snorting it. "Guh," he said while pinching the bridge of his nose. He took a shot of tequila, then squeezed a lime into his eye. "Oh, Christ," he muttered.

Again, the bar burst into cheers. Someone shook Nolan's shoulders and shouted, "You're an animal!"

Rodney didn't want to wait any longer. If he was forced to take part in the stupid tradition, he wanted to get it over with. He reached for the saltshaker. Tucker bumped him out of the way.

"We do it together," Tucker said. "Brothers in pain."

Rodney nodded. Maybe it would help spread the misery.

Tucker shook out two lines of salt, then slammed the shaker down. "Ready?"

"As I ever will be," Rodney said.

"Go!" cried Tucker.

The two men snorted their lines of salt. The burn in Rodney's sinuses was immediate, and he grabbed the bridge of his nose.

"Drink!" shouted Wiley. "Drink, you bastard!"

Rodney reached for the last shot glass. Tucker had already downed his tequila. He kicked the glass back and the oily liquor ran down this throat. Rodney grimaced.

Wiley repeatedly slapped the counter. "Lime! Lime! Lime!"

Rodney snatched the slice of fruit and looked toward the ceiling. He opened his right eye as wide as possible. The lime briefly hovered above his face. Rodney squeezed the small piece of fruit as hard as he could. Acidic juice dropped like small hydrogen bombs onto his cornea.

He dropped the lime and shoved his palm into his eye. The burning didn't stop. Rodney bent over as his heart raced. Had he just seared his retina forever?

The bar patrons shouted and clapped. Someone whistled loudly.

Rodney put his hands on the bar to steady himself. A new hard rock song started. Rodney didn't know this one either, but he picked up on the chorus, "Life / Birth / Blood / Doom."

Kaylee patted Rodney's back. "Relax. It's gonna sting for a while."

The bartender held out four wet rags. "Here you go, boys."

Each of the men grabbed one and held it to their affected eye. The cooling sensation helped Rodney immediately.

"You do this every year?" Rodney rasped.

"Hell yeah!" Wiley said. He shook Tucker by the neck. "It's a fucking tradition."

"One we could do without," Tucker muttered.

***

The group eventually moved outside. The guys winked at each other, the lot of them having one red eye a piece.

Rodney didn't want to drink with the Family. Dropping his guard created too many risks. Nolan, Wiley, and Tucker were halfway through their second beer while Rodney continued to sip his first. Even Kaylee drank faster than he did. With one tequila shot in him already, Rodney needed to be careful.

Wiley held his beer bottle aloft to prepare for a toast.

The others soon followed suit.

"To The Dilly-Dally," Wiley said, "the only safe place for a white man to drink anymore."

Nolan and Tucker clinked the bottles against Wiley's. Rodney hesitated briefly, but he tapped the neck of his bottle against the others.

Kaylee, however, lowered hers. "You're so full of shit," she said. "White men can drink wherever they want."

Wiley kicked his beer back. He shook his head as he swallowed. When he finished, he said, "Not true. Not even a little." He wiped his mouth with the back of his hand. "Everything now is trans-this or trans-that." Wiley waved his beer in the general direction of Omak. "Those LBGTQ fags are ruining everything. We can't even go to the bathroom with dudes anymore."

Kaylee raised her eyebrows. "You've had that problem?"

"Wiley has," Tucker said. "People have confused him with a pre-op woman for years."

Wiley dropped his hand below the table and grabbed his crotch. "I've got your pre-op right here."

"Doesn't sound like for much longer," Rodney said.

Tucker howled and Nolan spit his beer. Even Katie laughed. Wiley scowled, however.

As soon as the words left his mouth, Rodney regretted them. Of anyone in the Family, he knew better than to cross Wiley. The man was a loose cannon. Who knew what he might do?

Wiley lifted his chin toward Rodney's bottle. "You need a nipple for that, baby bird?"

"No."

"Then drink up."

"I'm not feeling well."

Wiley scrunched his face. "Aw. What's wrong, titty baby?"

Rodney shrugged. "I'm still dehydrated after all that time in the sun." It wasn't a total lie, but he didn't want to drink around the Family anymore.

"You gonna wuss out?" Wiley asked.

"Leave him alone," Tucker said. "You and the Old Man about drove him into the ground."

"What're you squawking about? We've all been there." Wiley eyed Kaylee. "Except maybe little girl over there."

The smile left Kaylee's face. "My initiation was worse than all of yours combined. You know it."

Wiley waved her off. "When we're through with him, we'll know we can trust him."

"I can trust him now," Tucker said.

"Well, I can't," Wiley said, "and neither can Saxon."

Rodney slowly turned his beer. He kept his mouth shut, knowing better than to make his situation worse by popping off.

"I'll give you this," Wiley said, "the Suicide Shot was a nice start." He tipped his bottle in Rodney's direction. "Better get started on your job."

The job, Rodney thought. He'd forgotten about it until that moment. He abruptly stood.

Kaylee held out her hand to stop him from leaving. "Hey. Don't do anything stupid."

Rodney nodded. "I won't."

She grabbed his wrist. "It's better to walk away from a bad job than to force one you don't feel good about."

"Mother hen," Wiley said, "let the baby bird go."

"Yeah, Mother," Nolan chided. "The boy's gonna do fine."

"You two," Kaylee said. "Knock off the mother bullshit

or I'm gonna cut you."

Tucker winked with his good eye. "Good luck, my friend. See you on the other side."

Rodney strode confidently out of The Dilly-Dally. His walk didn't convey how he truly felt.

3

Electric Mary

Rodney McCready pulled into Omak and drove along Main Street. The small city was less than ten minutes from the Farm and only five minutes from The Dilly-Dally Lounge.

Almost five thousand people lived in the unofficial hub of Okanogan County. Omak had a couple of grocery stores, a Super Walmart, and a Home Depot. It even had an Indian Casino. No other town in Okanogan County could boast of such a bounty. Some Canadians made frequent pilgrimages to shop in Omak, the border being only an hour to the north.

Rodney's right eye continued to burn because of the lime juice, and the world seemed slightly blurred because of it.

He pulled into an angled parking spot in front of a two-story building at the corner of Main and Bartlett. Several retail tenants filled the building's ground floor—a restaurant, an insurance company, and a salon. Apartments lined the upper level. Scaffolding stood in front of the southern part of the structure as workers replaced windows in the first apartment.

The landlord had made a big show of renovating the structure. He sent out letters to all the tenants and even got a write-up about his renovation in *The Omak-Okanogan Country Chronicle*, the local newspaper.

Rodney opened the truck's glove box and grabbed his

gun. He tucked it into the back of his jeans, underneath his T-shirt, and climbed out of the driver's seat. Rodney didn't bother locking the pickup; there was nothing left inside to steal.

He walked around the rear of the building and climbed the stairs to his apartment. Rodney lived in unit E, the second from the north end. He unlocked the front door and stepped inside. After closing the door, he paused and let his gaze flick about the apartment.

Was anything different? Had anything changed?

Nothing appeared to be missing, but that didn't mean someone hadn't been inside his apartment for a look around.

Rodney walked into the bathroom and found a small bottle of Visine in his medicine cabinet. He squeezed several drops into his right eye. Almost immediately, the burning sensation eased. He slipped the bottle into his pocket.

His cell phone sat on the kitchen counter, still attached to its charging cord. Rodney put his gun in a drawer, collected the phone, and left the apartment. He relocked the door and headed down to The Saddle Up Diner, the restaurant below his apartment.

The vinyl booth squeaked when Rodney slid into it. He chose the one nearest the window so he could look onto Main Street. A neon *Open* sign reflected off the inside pane. Overhead, some twangy country music played.

A plastic menu sat tucked between a container of ketchup and mustard, but Rodney didn't bother checking it. He'd been there often enough to know his choices.

Black and white photographs of cowboys and Native Americans hung on the walls above each booth. The pictures attempted to capture the beauty of the Old West.

In Rodney's eyes, the images looked hokey, though.

The Saddle Up Diner had probably been a nicer joint thirty years ago. Maybe even twenty. Now it seemed like a lot of other establishments in smaller Eastern Washington towns. Outdated and hanging on to life by its fingernails.

The only modern amenity the diner had was wireless internet. Rodney took advantage of it because his cell service was spotty in Omak.

A gray-haired server walked over. She wore a yellow T-shirt tucked into faded blue jeans. The logo on the shirt featured a woman on the back of a rearing horse with a plate balanced in her free hand. It read *Saddle Up for a Great Meal!*

"Getcha something, Rodney?" Her pen hovered above a notepad as she waited for his order.

"Evening, Carol. How about a Monte Cristo?"

"How about it?" she asked with a light chuckle.

Rodney often ordered the sandwich. He didn't know if it was the establishment's specialty, but he liked it better than anything else they had on the menu.

Carol jotted a note. "That it?"

Rodney glanced at the cook working the line. "Can Woody make the fries extra crispy?"

"If that's how you want 'em. Something to drink?"

"The usual."

Her pen hovered over the pad, and she stared at him.

"A Coke," he said, "but bring it with dinner."

"That's what I figured, but you need to say it so as I don't get it wrong." She scribbled her last note and wandered away.

Rodney called his phone to life and entered his four-digit code. The device automatically linked to the restaurant's wi-fi connection. Rodney flipped through a couple of screens until he found Intruder Defender Plus, the security monitoring app. He tapped it.

The screen changed and Rodney rotated the phone lengthwise. He had three cameras hidden in his apartment, which uploaded a video stream to the cloud. He'd purchased the cameras from a Best Buy superstore in Spokane. The cameras linked to the restaurant's wi-fi, a lucky fluke because of the proximity of Rodney's apartment.

He could access the video anywhere as long as he had good enough service. If Rodney were in a larger city such as Spokane, he could have done it without wi-fi. In North Central Washington, that wasn't an option.

No one could access his apartment without going through his front door. So, he only concerned himself with the first camera. He started that feed and watched it at eight times the normal speed. Nothing happened on the screen except the timer sped forward.

Whenever a customer entered the restaurant, Rodney glanced up and smiled. He'd then return his attention to his phone. He had repeated this process daily for weeks now, but no one had ever been in his apartment but him. Rodney never delayed watching the recorded video. The system only kept each packet for seventy-two hours. After that, it would auto-delete the old video unless he marked it for safekeeping.

"Here you go, hon."

Rodney paused the video as Carol slid his plate onto the table. She also put down his drink.

"Anything else?" she asked.

"I'm good."

She leaned closer. "What's wrong with your eye?"

"I poked myself."

"Doing what?"

"Not paying attention."

Carol shrugged. "That'll do it." She left to go help another customer.

The video was almost finished because the timer had reached the point when Rodney returned home. He felt reasonably safe he could stop it then, but he watched it until the end. It only took a few seconds more. When he confirmed no one had entered his apartment, Rodney put the phone down and took his first bite of dinner.

He happily chewed until two window installers entered the restaurant. The Hispanic men glanced in his direction, but they didn't return Rodney's smile. They approached the counter and ordered in hushed tones. Rodney checked on them with repeated glances over his shoulder.

The landlord had said the workers weren't supposed to be in his apartment for another week. What if they had access now? What if they moved the scaffolding and entered through his window, then returned the scaffolding to where it was now?

Rodney grabbed his phone and accessed the security monitoring app once more. He wanted to watch the camera in the living room. It would show if anyone entered through the second-story window. The video played at eight times its normal speed. Rodney chewed slowly, not wanting to finish his dinner too quickly.

"Whatcha watching?"

He looked up just as Electric Mary slid into the booth. She dropped her slouchy purse onto the seat next to her. Rodney covered the cell phone with his hand and slid it off the table.

"C'mon," she said. "Tell me." Her eyes carried a threat

of mischief. "Was it dirty?"

Mary was in her late twenties with voluptuous curves some women earn when they don't say no to their cravings. She had puffy lips and round cheeks which gave her a grown-up little girl look she'd likely never shake. Shiny dark hair cascaded over tanned shoulders. Even in his short time in Omak, he'd heard stories of how Mary had earned her nickname.

"Hey," she said. "What happened to your eye?"

"Nothing. I poked myself. What're you wearing?"

"This?" Mary tugged at the edges of a golden crocheted halter top, revealing milky white skin and dark areolas behind it. "It was my grandmother's. Can you believe it? Who knew Gram was such a babe?"

Dopamine spiked in Rodney's system even though he didn't want it. Even thinking about Electric Mary was a bad idea because of Wiley's affection for her. However, the woman was attractive, and it had been some time since Rodney had been with anyone.

Rodney had talked to Mary twice since they met at Kaylee's birthday party. Once at The Dilly-Dally and another time when he ran into her at the grocery store. She always seemed standoffish, like she was too good for him. Right now Mary wasn't acting aloof. He wondered what had changed.

Mary picked up the remaining portion of the Monte Cristo sandwich and bit into it. "What're you doing after this?" she asked through a mouthful of food.

"I don't know." Rodney shrugged. "Maybe workout or grab a beer at the Doghouse."

The Doghouse was a hole-in-the wall bar within walking distance of his apartment.

She swallowed her bite and ran her tongue over her

teeth. "Why don't we do both?" Mary bit into the sandwich again as trouble danced through her eyes.

Rodney's heart raced. "How's that?"

Mary tossed the remaining piece of sandwich onto the plate. "I just picked up a twelve-pack. It's in my car." She wiped her hands together. "Why don't we go up to your place and take out our frustrations on each other?"

"Who says I got frustrations?" Rodney asked. He heard the crack in his voice. Mary must have heard it, too.

She rolled her eyes. "Fine. Whatever. I'll take my frustrations out on you. It's been a week since I've gotten any and I'm about to go crazy."

"What about Wiley?"

Mary furrowed her brow. "What about him?"

"He's in love with you."

She slid out of the booth and tugged on the edges of her cut-off denim shorts. "If I worried about all the men in love with me, I'd never have time for anyone new. Apartment E, right?"

Rodney cocked his head. He wondered how she knew.

Mary reached into the booth and grabbed her purse. "I'll see you upstairs."

"Wait."

But she was gone and out of the restaurant. Rodney watched Mary's hips swing with unspoken promise as she strolled down the sidewalk. When she vanished around the corner, Rodney felt oddly disappointed.

Carol came over with the bill. "I'm supposing you want this now?"

Rodney looked up.

"Word of advice." She lowered her voice. "You should probably be more discreet with your business. This being a small town and all."

When Carol walked away, Rodney glanced around the restaurant.

The remaining customers watched him with a mixture of curiosity and astonishment.

***

Mary waited outside Rodney's apartment door. She held her droopy purse in her left hand and a twelve-pack of Pabst in her right. "I thought you might ditch me."

"Why would I do that?"

"Maybe you're afraid I'll bite."

"I'm not afraid of that." He stuck the key in the lock.

"You should be. I also scratch and leave bruises." She lifted an eyebrow. "If you're lucky, that is."

Rodney pushed the door open, and Mary slipped by. Her bare shoulders and waist immediately sent a thrill through him.

"This is a bad idea," he muttered.

"What's that?"

He pulled the door closed. Mary handed him the case of beer and dropped her purse on the floor. She headed deeper into the apartment but stopped at the first open door—his bedroom. She leaned in but didn't leave the hallway.

More dopamine coursed through Rodney's system as he studied Mary's butt in those cutoff denim shorts.

"Huh," she said.

"What?"

Mary pulled back into the hallway and shook her head. "It's nothing."

"No, seriously."

Her brow furrowed. "You got like a kid's bed."

"It's a twin size." Rodney suddenly felt defensive and added, "It's all I need."

"It's fine," she said. "You must not have many guests."

Before he could respond, Mary wandered off into the rest of the apartment. There wasn't much for her to see, but she inspected everything as if she were a child visiting a toy store.

Rodney's furniture came from various thrift shops in the county. When he purchased the items, he wasn't trying to develop a theme; he was simply answering questions of utility. Can I sleep on this? Can I sit there? Will this help me make a meal? Above all, the items couldn't be too nice. A guy without steady employment couldn't have anything nice or it'd raise questions.

"You read?" Mary asked.

"Some."

She pushed over a stack of paperbacks on the coffee table. Mary bent to consider several of the titles. Rodney clutched the case of beer to his chest as he once more appreciated her butt.

"You've read all these?" she asked.

"Not yet," Rodney said absently.

The denim cutoffs rode so high up Mary's backside they left little to his imagination, yet still he tried.

Mary picked up a paperback, Nevada Barr's *High Country*, and briefly considered it. Her gaze flitted about the room. "You got no TV."

"Can't afford one."

"This is how you live?" She waggled the book. "Reading for fun?"

"Ain't so bad."

Mary's eyes narrowed. "Look at you, Mr. Big Brain. I haven't read anything since high school. You probably think I'm dumb."

"I don't think that."

"No?" She tossed the paperback onto the table. "Gimme that beer."

She snatched the case from him and headed toward the kitchen.

Rodney's wits returned. Messing around with Electric Mary was wrong, he reminded himself. He needed to get her out of his apartment. "You should probably go." He flinched at how weak his protest sounded.

"What's the hurry?" She put the beer on the counter. "I just got here."

He shook his head. He should have been more forceful.

Mary pulled open the drawer that contained his gun. She pulled back as if threatened by it. She immediately closed the drawer. "Sorry."

"What're you looking for?" Rodney asked.

"Snacks."

"In the cabinet below."

He should have told her to leave, but he really didn't want her to go. His body vibrated with anticipation of what might soon happen. Rodney only knew the woman by reputation, but here she was, in his apartment, like they were old friends.

Mary opened the lower cabinet and squatted. The denim shorts rode up again. Even though she had a terrible reputation, she had a wonderful body. Her hand dangled over the side of a cabinet door. "This all you got?"

"I'm not here much."

Her head bobbled from side to side as she studied the meager food choices. "What do you do with your time?"

"Look for work."

"Heard you were hanging out on the Farm."

"People talk too much."

She laughed. "What else they got to do around here? You don't have Pringles?"

"Only what's there."

"Too bad." She closed the cabinet door and stood. Her fingers slipped inside her shorts and tugged them into place. When she faced him, she adjusted the crocheted halter top, revealing the untanned skin of her breasts again. "I thought your place would've been nicer."

Rodney tried to swallow, but his mouth had gone dry. It had been almost two years since he'd been with a woman, before his last stint in prison. His girlfriend had moved on while he was incarcerated, and he hadn't found anyone to hook up with since then. It was like the world had conspired to keep him celibate.

Mary studied him briefly, then nodded with satisfaction. "I heard you and Tucker did time together."

"Some."

She picked up the case of beer and turned to the refrigerator. "Where was that?"

"Coyote Ridge."

Mary shoved the box inside. "Where's that again?"

"Connell."

"In there long?" She ripped the case open.

"Thirteen months."

She looked over her shoulder and caught him staring at her ass. "Get out on good behavior?"

Rodney cleared his throat. "The full bit."

Mary pulled out a single can and closed the door. She popped it open and took a healthy swallow. After wiping her mouth, she extended the beer. "To friends."

Rodney accepted the can and lifted it to his lips.

Mary tugged the halter top over her head. Her milky-white breasts bounced as they fell back into place. They stood in stark contrast to the rest of her tanned body. "So," Mary said, "we gonna try out that little kid's bed or we gonna do it on the couch?"

***

"Sorry about your bed," Mary said.

Rodney stared at the ceiling. "Don't be."

The two sat naked, side-by-side on the couch, with their feet resting on the edge of the coffee table. Sweat covered them both. After the frame broke, it left the bed at an unusable angle. They moved into the living room.

"Christ, it's hot in here," Mary said. "You need a fan or air-conditioning or something."

Rodney grunted. Now that the act was over, regret filled him. He shouldn't have slept with Mary. Wiley had feelings for her. This would certainly cause problems. Rodney had gone through too much to risk it for some sex—no matter how good it was.

Mary rolled her head on the back of the couch and studied him. "You were better than I expected."

Even though Rodney had just chastised himself for messing around with her, Mary's comment stung. Had she expected him to be a lousy lay? Rodney stared at her.

"Don't look at me like I kicked your dog," she said. "It's just I've never been with a reader before. I dunno how you guys are. I thought maybe you'd wanna talk through it or something."

"Talk?"

"Or cuddle or whatnot." Mary frowned. "Stop looking at me like I hurt your feelings."

"You didn't hurt my feelings."

41

"I was trying to give you a compliment." She stood but didn't bother to hide her nakedness. Mary was a woman confident in her form.

"Where you going?" he asked.

"The bathroom."

Rodney started to stand, but she held up a hand.

"Stay there." Mary grabbed the half-empty beer from the coffee table and gave it to him. "We're not done. Round two is happening when I get back."

She padded off and the bathroom door closed.

Rodney cupped the can of beer and thought about Wiley again. The man hadn't liked Rodney from the moment they met at Kaylee's birthday party. Tucker had said Wiley had an inferiority complex. He hadn't used those exact words, but that's what Tucker meant. He told Rodney, whenever someone new entered Saxon's inner circle, Wiley felt threatened. Right now, Rodney was the target of Wiley's angst.

Instead of screwing around with Electric Mary, Rodney should have spent his time trying to figure out how he was going to raise ten grand. Saxon wanted him to pull a job. No doubt it would have to be big enough to make the news, otherwise the Family wouldn't believe it.

Rodney absently sipped the beer. It was warm now.

The bathroom door opened. Mary padded through the apartment but didn't return to the living room.

"What're you doing?" Rodney asked.

"Grabbing my purse."

"For?" He sipped the beer and stared at the ceiling.

A truck raced along Main Street. Its engine continued to roar into the distance. Rodney still hadn't gotten used to the sounds of vehicles speeding up and down the road at all hours.

He tilted his head, listening for the sounds of Mary. "Hey."

"Hold your horses."

Rodney heard the refrigerator open and close a moment later. Mary returned with a beer. She flopped onto the couch next to him. With one hand, she pulled the coffee table a few inches closer. Mary put her feet up on it, then cracked open the new can of beer before sipping it.

"What'd you need your purse for?" Rodney asked.

"Girl stuff."

He finished drinking the remaining warm beer and put the empty on the coffee table.

Mary handed him the cold Pabst. "Got a date for the Suicide Race?"

Rodney shook his head. The Omak Stampede started the next day, and the Suicide Race was on Saturday. The annual rodeo was the talk of the town. Supposedly, a bunch of riders guided their horses over a cliff, across the Okanogan River, and into the fairgrounds.

"Me, neither," Mary said. "We should go together."

Rodney knew what he should say, but he said the opposite. "Okay."

"Hopefully, we don't get a bunch of protesters this year."

"That happened before?"

She scoffed. "Almost every year now. A bunch of west-side namby-pambies come to the rodeo and try to shut it down because of the horses. Fucking liberals need to stay on their side of the mountains."

Rodney didn't say anything. Not because he had an opinion about the Stampede, the Suicide Race, or the west-side liberals. Instead, he stared at Mary's bare breasts.

A smile spread across her lips. "Ready for another go?"

"We shouldn't," Rodney said. His words carried little conviction.

"Why shouldn't we?" She reached into his lap and wriggled her fingers. "Don't say Wiley, because he's never gonna have another shot with me."

Rodney stared into her eyes as she continued to move her hand.

Her smile twisted into a smirk. "You don't have a good reason we shouldn't do it again, do you?"

"Not really."

Electric Mary lowered her head, and Rodney knew damn well his troubles were only beginning.

4

The Puppet Master

The alarm sounded at six. Rodney grabbed his phone and silenced it. He lay in bed, letting sleep overwhelm him again in its comforting embrace. A moment later, he opened his eyes.

The job.

He slipped out of bed and felt a slight headache—the lingering effects of too many beers. Rodney preferred to drink vodka if he was going to drink at all. That liquor didn't seem to give him a headache the way beer did. He slipped on his underwear and walked into the kitchen. Rodney poured a glass of water at the tap and gulped it.

On the counter was a note from Mary. *See you Saturday!* she wrote. It also included an address on South Index Street. He slid the note off the counter and into the drawer where his gun was.

How many hours did he have left to produce a job? It was about four yesterday when Saxon told him he had forty-eight. So, he'd already wasted fourteen of them doing nothing.

Rodney's eyes cut to the living room couch. Not nothing, he corrected. He'd spent a chunk of those fourteen hours tangled up with Electric Mary. In other words, he made his life immensely more difficult.

"Way to go, dumb ass," he muttered to himself.

Now, he had to worry about Wiley Jones. If the man found out about his tryst with Mary, who knew how he'd react? Rodney didn't want to find out.

But his first problem was pulling a job with a $10,000 payday. Those types of scores didn't grow on trees.

Rodney narrowed his eyes. There was something bigger involved with the job than just the money.

Saxon had said, "I don't trust you." The Old Man certainly meant it in the context of Rodney proving his skills. Yet the job was also to show he was trustworthy enough to be a member of the Family. That Rodney could be entrusted with certain information and keep his mouth shut if the time ever came.

To pull a job of this magnitude in such a short amount of time, Rodney needed help.

He found his jeans on the bedroom floor. His cell phone was in a front pocket. Rodney dialed a number he committed to memory. He only put numbers into his phone that he didn't care if the entire world knew.

The call was answered on the third ring. "This better be good," a gruff male voice answered.

"I'm sorry to wake you, but I need some help."

"That doesn't sound good."

"It's not," Rodney said. "Can we meet?"

"Can it wait?"

"Not really. I'm under a time crunch."

The man sighed. "Fine. The designated place. At eleven."

"See you then."

Rodney hung up and deleted the call from his phone's history.

***

When he was in prison, Rodney learned to kill time by

reading and exercising. Books were a great diversion when his mind was unsettled. However, if Rodney sat around for three hours now, he would have worried about the job and the bad choices he'd recently made.

He needed to move.

Rodney dressed for a jog and left the apartment. He strapped on his digital watch as he walked down the stairs. He only wore it while running. It wasn't fancy. In fact, it was the cheapest one available at the local pharmacy. Rodney only used the clock function to monitor how long he'd be out.

He zigzagged through Omak until he made it to a path trending along the Okanogan River. He ran northbound on it until it petered out near Juniper Street. Rodney kept jogging, twisting and turning through neighborhoods, making his way northeast through the small city.

Whenever a vehicle drove by, Rodney lifted his hand in a friendly greeting. Most drivers returned the gesture.

Rodney wasn't a great runner. He was more of a plodder, simply putting one foot in front of the other until he reached a destination. He never ran for pace or distance. It was only to get outside and burn off nervous energy. Rodney started running after his first prison stretch. Most guys couldn't wait to get back to what they were doing before they went in—drugs, women, or the other sources of their trouble. Rodney wanted to find some peace.

He found it with a pair of running shoes.

At the start of this run, his mind flooded with concerns about Electric Mary. Rodney knew he shouldn't have gotten involved with her, but his regrets were mixed with memories of carnal delights. He wanted to think, if Mary showed up at his apartment again, he'd have the smarts to say no to her advances. However, Rodney knew himself—

he'd never say no to a woman who could do what Mary did.

The initial hint of pain in his legs usually showed up early, less than a quarter mile into every run. That was Rodney's mind playing tricks as a way to get him to quit. He always focused on his breathing to work through the discomfort. Things smoothed out after that.

Worries of Electric Mary soon faded away. So did any tangential thoughts of the Old Man and the Family.

Rodney jogged along Koala Drive and the morning sun baked him. Running in the heat was a test of his willpower. In the later hours of the day, he'd likely quit. He knew himself well enough to admit that. The morning temperature was still in the low 80s and it wasn't too bad.

There wasn't much to see in this part of Omak. A few buildings. A hotel. None of it mattered, though, since Rodney wasn't sightseeing. He was running to be free. The world opened to him now, and everything felt possible.

Rodney had never competed in a race before. Oh, he'd outrun some cops, and that felt good. He'd sprinted from guys looking to do him harm. He thought about races like the one Spokane held back in May. Lots of citizens took part in Bloomsday every year. Rodney had thought about doing it before, but always talked himself out of it. He was sure he could do the run since it was only seven and a half miles long. However, he didn't want to be clustered in among thirty thousand participants.

Being in prison, confined in such small quarters, with all those other men, was bad enough. He didn't want to be jammed together with so many people while doing something he loved. Running afforded him tranquility. He didn't want that tainted because of all those citizens.

Rodney checked his watch. He'd been running for

forty-five minutes.

He made sure the lanes were clear and crossed the road. Then he turned around and headed home. His shoes slapped the pavement and his side throbbed. He inhaled deeply to control the aches in his body.

There was plenty of time for him to get home, grab a shower, and eat some breakfast.

Then Rodney would drive to the designated meeting place.

***

Moses Lake was two hours south of Omak via Highway 17. Rodney McCready grew up there, but he hadn't returned until recently. That's when he discovered he still had a fondness for the place. It felt odd for Rodney to confront those emotions because he hated Moses Lake all those years ago.

To be fair, he jumbled up his feelings about the town with those concerning his father. He dropped out of high school in the eleventh grade to escape the area. In reality, he was running from his family's legacy.

It seemed everyone in town had known Rodney's father, a career politician who put his aspiration for power over the care of his family. The McCready name once carried a lot of weight. Rodney's two sisters loved the attention their family got. Rodney despised it.

His father died ten years ago of emphysema during one of Rodney's prison stretches. After that, his mother immediately moved to Arizona with the lover everyone had pretended not to know about. His sisters never called the prison to check on Rodney, and he didn't know where they lived now. No relative ever phoned during the holidays or sent a birthday card—not even his mother. Rodney supposed he preferred it that way—no connections, no regrets.

On his recent trips to Moses Lake, Rodney never considered driving by his childhood home. As far as he was concerned, the two-story house on Bertram Way could burn to the ground, along with all its memories.

Newer construction was everywhere in the Central Washington community: housing developments, apartment complexes, and retail shopping centers. It was as if money and shoppers had flooded the area. Who were these people? Rodney wondered. Where had they all come from? Why did they find Moses Lake so desirable an area to live?

He turned left on Broadway Avenue and continued south into an older part of town. Along this stretch of road, landlords renovated once dilapidated structures into coffeehouses, brewpubs, and holistic studios. The whole town was trying to change its image, Rodney thought. Like it was trying to be a Spokane knockoff or worse—a Seattle suburb.

Rodney pulled into the parking lot of the Cosmos Diner and parked next to two Harley-Davidson motorcycles. On the gas tank of each bike was a custom-painted skull shrouded in smoke.

The restaurant was a local mainstay and had changed little since Rodney lived there as a kid. It had a curved roof and a rocked-wall exterior. Inside the establishment, two small televisions hung behind the bar and some '80s pop music played from a jukebox.

A thick-shouldered man in jeans and a leather vest sat at the bar, eating a hamburger. A patch covered the back of the leather cut. It featured the same logo from the bikes outside. A rocker above the patch read *Wasted Souls*. The lower rocker read *Spokane, WA*. Even though Rodney was related to the man, the two didn't acknowledge each other.

Further into the bar sat an older, heavyset man. A black leather cap compressed the top of his long gray hair, and his gray beard hid most of his face. He watched Rodney approach. Two glasses of beer sat on the table; the one in front of the older man was half-empty.

"You're late," Booster said.

Rodney furrowed his brow. He had arrived a couple of minutes early for their meeting.

"If I beat you here," the older man said, "you're late. Know the rules, Prospect." Booster lowered his voice even further. "Why'd you ask for a meet?"

Rodney whispered, "I gotta pull a job."

A server approached with two plates. She was a tall woman with a pleasant demeanor. "Cheeseburgers with fries."

Booster lifted his arms off the table. "I ordered for you."

Rodney didn't like cheese on his burgers, but he said nothing except, "Thanks." No one questioned the president of the Wasted Souls, especially someone trying to become a member of the motorcycle club.

The server suddenly smiled. "Rodney?"

It took a moment for him to recognize her. "Denise?"

"Oh my God, how many years has it been?"

"Twenty, I'd guess."

She reached out but stopped short of touching his shoulder. "You look good." Her eyes flashed to Booster. "I'm sorry. I'm interrupting your lunch." Her gaze bounced between the two men. "Will there be anything else?"

"Another beer," Booster said.

She nodded, then turned back to Rodney. "It was nice to see you."

"You, too," he said.

Denise wandered off.

"That going to be a problem?" Booster asked.

"I don't think so."

"Don't let it be." The Wasted Soul's president picked up his burger and bit into it. Rodney did the same. He wasn't hungry, but a man in his position mirrored the actions of his superiors. As a prospect, everyone in the club was his better.

"Good fucking burger," Booster muttered through a mouthful of food.

Rodney nodded as he chewed. It was good, but he wasn't sure how he'd get it all down.

The club president swallowed, then pointed at Rodney with his burger. "Why do you have to pull a job?"

"Saxon doesn't trust me."

Booster bit into his sandwich again. He grunted while he ate.

A song came on the radio that Rodney had heard before. It grated on him because the female singer kept wailing about "Manic Monday." Rodney thought the song was stupid for many reasons, not the least of which it was Thursday. He stuffed a couple of French fries into his mouth.

"Saxon isn't making you do this to show you got *cajones*. He knows you were in the can with what's-his-nuts."

"Tucker."

"Yeah, him. So he knows you aren't afraid of getting your hands dirty. He thinks there's a puppet master, someone pulling your strings."

Rodney cocked his head. "He knows about us?"

Booster waved what remained of his burger. "He thinks you're working for the cops."

"Why would he think that?"

"Because he's a suspicious prick. Some unknown shows up and rekindles a prison friendship as a way to join the Family. What's he gonna think?"

Rodney lifted his burger but paused before biting it. "That's not how you think about me, is it?"

Booster cocked an eyebrow. "I'm no more trusting than Saxon. Prospects have to earn our confidence. That's why we make you do what you do." The president lifted his chin toward the man at the bar. "Besides, Axel is your cousin. He vouched for you."

"When do you know I'm good to go?"

"It ain't a science." Booster shoved some fries into his mouth and spoke while he chewed. "Don't worry about it. You got a long way to go to prove yourself. Cousins don't mean shit. It's club before family. Remember that."

For a moment, Rodney wondered if Booster meant family with a capital "F."

Denise returned with a glass of beer and set it on the table next to Booster's plate. "How are things?" She smiled at Rodney as she asked the question.

"They're fine," the club president said flatly. "We'll holler if we need anything else."

Denise caught the tone and nodded. "Enjoy your meal." She wandered off.

"Back to Saxon," Booster said. "He say anything about the type of job it has to be?"

"Just I gotta bring back ten grand."

"Why that amount?"

"He said I had to spread it among the Family. Two

grand a piece."

Booster's lip curled. "The Family is a lot bigger than that. He's testing you. Seeing how much you know. What'd you say when he told you to pull the job?"

"I said okay. I'd do it."

Booster crinkled his nose and looked toward the ceiling. "Pulling the job is as important as showing up with the money."

"That's what I was thinking."

The president's gaze slowly lowered back to Rodney. "That's what you thought?"

"Yeah."

"Then why'n the fuck did you call me?" Booster glared at him. "You want my help or not?"

Rodney should have kept his mouth shut.

"I didn't need to drag my ass out here. I had plenty of shit to do today. I should let you figure out how to pull this job on your own."

"Hey, man, I'm sorry."

"One word from me—" Booster pointed at the man at the bar. "Axel will burn your cut. I'll make him do it because he vouched for you, because you two are family. Teach you both a lesson. Got it? You'll never get your patch. You'll never have existed with the Souls. He'll carry your stain forever. You hearing me?"

Rodney lifted an apologetic hand. "Booster."

"You need to remember where you fit in this hierarchy. You're at the bottom. No, you're lower than that. You're whale shit."

"I got it."

Booster dropped the last bite of his burger and picked up his half-full glass of beer. He emptied its contents in two big gulps. He set the glass down and wiped his mouth with his hand. "So."

"I apologize."

The president stroked his beard. "How long have you got to pull this job?"

"About thirty hours."

"Not much time."

Rodney nodded. He figured he didn't need to tell the man about the lost hours with Electric Mary.

Booster crossed his arms and stared ahead. His eyes narrowed and widened several times. It unnerved Rodney, and he reached for his glass of beer.

"I'll tell you what," Booster said calmly.

Rodney let go of the beer and waited for the president's next words. They didn't come immediately.

Booster's jaw moved about as if he was still trying to decide something. Finally, he said, "You're gonna hit one of our legitimate joints."

Rodney leaned in and whispered. "What?"

"You heard me. We'll make sure it's loaded with some cash. Shoot it up and make it messy. Understand? That way we can report it to the cops and the insurance company. It'll make the news, too. Once that happens, Saxon'll have his confirmation, and you'll get in good with the Family."

Rodney nodded. "All right. Yeah. Thanks."

"Don't thank me yet. You still gotta do your part." Booster stood. "Eat your burger. I'll be back."

The president ambled over to Axel. Rodney wished he could hear what they were talking about, but the restaurant's bouncy music drowned out their conversation.

Rodney looked away because he didn't want to be caught staring at the two men. He bit into the cheeseburger and pretended to be hungry.

He still didn't understand why Booster and the Souls wanted him to infiltrate the Family. From what he knew, Saxon mostly operated as a waypoint for smugglers taking stuff in and out of Canada. The Family pulled occasional jobs, but Rodney didn't know what kind. He really felt in the dark about the whole assignment.

Regardless, a smuggling waypoint seemed like a strange place for the motorcycle club to be interested in. Rodney didn't know everything about the Souls' operation, either. He figured there was something bigger at play between the two organizations.

Right now, Rodney had a simple mission—get in with the Family. If that happened, he'd get patched in with the Souls. Then he could finally straighten out his life.

Booster returned to his chair. After he sat, the club president slid a piece of paper across the table. "Here you go. Hit it before five tonight. That's when they close."

Rodney didn't have his watch on anymore. He searched the restaurant for a clock and found one above the bar. It was almost half-past eleven.

"Not much time to plan," Rodney said.

"What's there to plan?" Booster asked. "Go there, hit it, and take the cash. Simple."

"All right."

Booster leaned in. "Make it loud," he whispered. "This has got to make the news. Understand?"

"Got it."

The president of the club stood. "Pay the check and deal with the server." He headed for the exit.

Axel slid off his bar stool and followed Booster. He paused at the door and motioned for Rodney to meet him outside. Then both men disappeared into the sunlight.

Rodney stared at the slip of paper. *Roses are Red—*

Davenport was the only thing written on it.

Denise returned to the table. "Your friend left?"

"I'll take the bill when you get a chance."

She crossed her arms and smiled. "Rodney McCready. I can't believe it's really you. I just moved back, and it's like my third day here. You're the first one of the old gang I've seen. What have you been up to?"

Rodney didn't want to encourage the conversation any further. He also didn't want to say anything memorable. Sitting at a table with a member of the Wasted Souls was already going to stick in Denise's memory.

"Bouncing around," Rodney said. "Odd jobs mostly."

"You're back, too?" Her smile broadened and hope filled her eyes.

"Just visiting."

She wasn't in a hurry to return to her work, and Rodney didn't want to be rude. He and Denise had been friendly in high school. She was one of the few people he had fond memories of. He reached into his pocket and pulled a fifty from his pocket. He laid it on the table.

"I hate to run," he said.

Her eyes flicked to the bill. "Wait. I'll get your change."

Rodney held up a hand. "It's okay. I'll stop in later so we can chat some more."

"I'd like that." Denise touched his arm. "I'd like that a lot."

He headed for the door. Rodney had no intention of ever returning to the Cosmos Diner.

***

Rodney stepped out of the restaurant in time to see Booster roar away on his Harley.

Axel leaned on the seat of his bike. His arms were crossed, and he watched Rodney approach. "I hope you know what you're doing."

"I'm trying to get in good with the Family."

"That's not what I'm talking about."

Rodney stopped in front of his cousin. "Then what? The server? I blew her off."

"The club, man." Concern flashed through Axel's eyes. "Is all this worth it?"

Rodney didn't understand what his cousin was asking. "You mean the patch?"

Even though they were the same age, the two men had never been close. Rodney's aunt lived in Walla Walla where she raised Axel and his sister. When Axel graduated high school, he gravitated toward Spokane, much like Rodney had. They both found trouble to their liking.

They grew up seeing each other mostly at family events on the holidays or during the summer. Rodney's parents would visit Walla Walla, or Axel's mom would come up to Moses Lake.

Axel pushed off the bike. "I mean—" He looked away from Rodney. "I guess I'm asking if you're okay?"

"I'm fine."

"No trouble?"

"With Saxon?" Rodney shook his head. "I'm good outside of this job I've gotta do. Did Booster tell you about it?"

Axel nodded. His eyes returned to Rodney. "Mom asks how you're doing."

"Yeah? How's she?"

"Responding to treatment." Axel shrugged a single shoulder. "Too early to tell if it's making a difference."

"I'm sorry."

Axel looked toward the blue sky. "She'll come through. She's a fighter."

"Yeah, she is."

"You hear anything from your mom?"

Rodney rolled down his lower lip. "Haven't heard from her in ages. I don't try, though."

"That's too bad." Axel sighed. "Family's important."

"Club over family," Rodney said, parroting Booster's words.

Axel rolled his eyes. "We're talking our mothers, not our wives or girlfriends. There's a difference."

Rodney nodded.

"Anyway," Axel said, "I just wanted to make sure you're okay."

"I'm fine."

"So you said. Hey, isn't it your birthday tomorrow?"

Rodney raised an eyebrow. "You remembered."

"Not enough to get you anything." Axel flicked his hand. "But happy birthday."

"Thank you." Rodney patted his pocket. "What's this place I'm supposed to hit?"

"That's above my pay grade. I'm not paid to know stuff."

Rodney thumbed over his shoulder. "I better get going. Got places to be."

"You be careful."

Rodney headed for his truck. He glanced back at Axel who now stared at the ground.

"Hey," Rodney said. "What about you? You okay?"

"Yeah. Just hungover."

"I know the feeling."

Rodney waved goodbye and climbed into his truck. He backed out of the parking stall as Axel climbed onto his motorcycle.

5

The Greenhouse Incident

Rodney approached the quiet community of Davenport, an hour and a half northeast of Moses Lake. He'd driven there immediately after his meeting with Booster and Axel. Rodney had been to the small farm town before. It was hard to traipse around Eastern Washington and not know about it.

The little burg sat on Highway 2, a major route from Spokane to Central Washington. The speed limit dropped to 20 MPH on Davenport's outskirts. Rodney never stopped there for anything other than an occasional tank of gas.

At the western edge of town, an electronic sign stood on a small flatbed trailer. Above the sign was a placard that read *Courtesy of Washington State Patrol*. Its digital readout repeatedly flashed red—32 MPH. Rodney lowered his speed further and scanned the road ahead for waiting patrol cars. The last thing he needed was an overeager cop, or worse, some zealous trooper.

Not seeing any law, Rodney relaxed. Few people moved about the businesses lining Highway 2. There were cars in the parking lot of the town's Safeway, but it seemed most everyone stayed inside to beat the heat. Even the town's gas station appeared deserted. Davenport's quiet nature suited Rodney fine if Booster's lead turned out true.

Why wouldn't it? It was a Wasted Souls' business.

Rodney didn't know where it was. All he had was the

business name—Roses are Red. How hard could it be to find in this sleepy town? Rodney could pull out his phone and look up his destination if he could get decent coverage. However, he felt confident about locating it without the help of technology. The town wasn't that big.

He drove east through Davenport, scanning the buildings lining the major thoroughfare. Rodney glanced at a road sign. Highway 2 was also the town's Morgan Street.

Rodney imagined a florist needed to be along the main retail hub, which clearly Morgan Street was. However, most shops were closed. The town's heyday was long in its rearview mirror. How could a florist survive in a place like Davenport? How many farmers were buying flowers for their wives? Wouldn't they just grow that shit?

He reached the far end of town in a couple of minutes and turned into the parking lot of a cannabis retailer. Rodney headed back the way he came, worried he might have missed the business. His head swiveled from side to side until he reached the Safeway. The florist wasn't on the main drag.

Rodney grunted. Why didn't Booster just give him the damn address? Maybe he didn't know it. That was the simplest explanation. Or perhaps Booster wanted to make Rodney work to find it. He was still a prospect, after all. The Souls wouldn't hand anything to him on a platter.

He continued for a few moments and turned around at the regional airport. This time, Rodney entered the neighborhood north of Highway 2. There were a couple of businesses in the area but nothing remotely like a florist. He went through the neighborhood and passed a church, an apartment complex, before finding the town's hospital. Rodney quickly covered the north side of town, but it didn't leave him feeling positive. It left him worried.

Maybe he'd misread Booster's note. *Roses are Red—Davenport.*

Could Davenport have a different meaning? Was there a Davenport Street somewhere? Was it back in Moses Lake? Or was it in Spokane where the Souls were based?

Rodney crossed Highway 2 and entered the south part of town. He should have just pulled his phone out and checked his coverage. If he had any, he could search for the business name. Rodney was mad at himself now. Had he driven ninety minutes the wrong way to find a florist that didn't exist? Goddamn Booster. Why wouldn't he just tell him?

There were several businesses south of the highway, including a retirement home, but this part of town was clearly a residential area.

Rodney struggled to control his impatience. He gripped the steering wheel as he slowly drove by the town's high school. When he reached the west end of town, he saw the fairgrounds, and shouted, "Fuck!" The outburst didn't ease his frustration.

He continued southbound and now banged his fist on the steering wheel. He left the radio off since he didn't want to be distracted by any music.

"Why am I even doing this?" he asked himself. He sat up higher in the seat so he could see his reflection in the rearview mirror. "You know why, dumb ass." Rodney dropped back down.

Occasionally, someone was outside in their yard, and they noticed Rodney. This often elicited a wave from the homeowner, which he politely returned, even though he felt like cursing at them.

Courtesy wasn't remembered in this part of the state.

Rudeness was.

Eventually, Rodney passed the local grade school and found an industrial area. Beyond these few buildings was nothing but a mixture of scrub and farmland. He'd have to give up soon.

Rodney was on Monroe Street, at the southernmost edge of town, when he found it.

"Finally," he muttered.

A large greenhouse sat perpendicular to the road. Many of its windows were open and sunlight glinted off them. A white sign with dual posts was positioned near the small parking lot. It read *Roses are Red—a private greenhouse.* Underneath the business name, was a smaller sign—*By Appointment Only.* Two newer pickup trucks sat at the front. A chain-link fence surrounded its lot. Bags of soil and other gardening items lay in the baking sun.

Rodney continued past the business and discovered a highway intersecting the street a couple of blocks away.

That's probably why the Wasted Souls chose a building like that to launder their money. It was out of the way, and no one would think to look twice. If the Souls needed a quick escape route, they could jump on the highway.

Rodney felt himself calming down now that he'd found the greenhouse. He drove away from Roses are Red and parked near a grain silo. No one was around. Rodney pulled out his phone to see if he could make a call. Unfortunately, he didn't have service. It was an unfortunate byproduct of his prepaid plan. He'd gotten used to it, so he didn't get mad. He could have subscribed to a monthly service like a citizen if he wanted to let the cops track his every movement. Rodney would rather remain anonymous and not have excellent cell coverage.

He also couldn't use the GPS service to see where the

nearby highway went. In reality, it wasn't important. Rodney knew the road went south. All he had to do was get away from Davenport without being pursued by any cops.

Booster had said to make the job noisy and messy.

Rodney reached over, opened the glove box, and pulled out his gun. There was no need to rack the slide like they did in the movies. There was always a round in the chamber. He tucked the gun into the back of his jeans.

It was time to rob his club.

***

Rodney returned to Monroe Street and parked next to the other two pickups in front of the greenhouse. He turned off the engine before slipping out of the truck. Normally, he'd leave it running, but this was a different kind of heist. They knew he was coming. Rodney expected whoever was inside to play along.

A camera at the east edge of the building pointed in his direction. Rodney kept his head low and his shoulders hunched as he walked as nonchalantly as he could to the entrance. Another camera pointed down at the front of the greenhouse. A third camera was directed toward the west side of the parking field.

Windows surrounded the building and framed its roof. Even its door contained a large window, but looking through it, everything appeared distorted, like peering into a clear lake after a boat had passed by. Rodney wondered if the door's window was plastic instead of glass. If that were the case, were all the windows plastic?

Rodney tried the front door handle, but it didn't turn.

By appointment only, he reminded himself. A handwritten sign next to the door read *Ring bell for service.* Rodney did so. He also knocked on the metal door frame for added emphasis.

The sun beat down on Rodney as he stood next to the greenhouse. It seemed extra hot there.

A noisy car headed along Monroe Street, and Rodney glanced over his shoulder. Hispanic music thumped through the open windows of a lowered Honda. None of the occupants looked in Rodney's direction.

He turned back to the door in time to see a shadow approaching from the inside. He stepped to the side as it opened.

A sweaty, white male with short black hair and a trimmed beard stuck his head out. "You need an appointment."

"It's my anniversary," Rodney said.

"We're not that kind of place."

The guy pushed the door wider to reveal himself. He had beauty muscles—thick shoulders, bulging biceps, and a slim waist. Guys in prison developed the same look when they spent too much time with the weights. He wore a red T-Shirt, blue shorts, and white tennis shoes. A revolver in a holster rode on his left hip.

"I'll pay double," Rodney said.

"Listen, pal—" The guy had one hand on the door and the other on the frame. It was supposed to be an intimidating pose, but he'd made a mistake. He kept his hands occupied. "Take your business elsewhere. We don't need it."

Rodney pulled the gun from underneath his shirt and jammed it into the man's gut.

The big man let go of the door and shuffled back. "Hey, now. Take it easy."

Rodney followed him inside. He closed the door and locked it.

It was hotter inside the greenhouse. Humid, too. The place stunk like an old woman at church. Rows of potted roses lined the entire structure. At the far end of the building was an enclosed office.

Annoying country music floated through the building. Rodney didn't know who the female singer was. He never listened to the stuff.

"Who else is here?" Rodney asked.

"No one."

"There's a second truck. Don't make me shoot you."

The big man motioned over his shoulder. "Zeke, but he's in the head."

"What do I call you?"

"Jed."

Perspiration popped out on Rodney's forehead, and a trickle of sweat ran down his armpit.

"All right, Jed," Rodney said. "Take your gun out with your opposite hand and put it on the ground."

The big man reached for his gun.

"Like it's an egg," Rodney added.

Jed slowed his movement. He pulled his gun out from the holster with his right hand and set it on the ground.

Rodney motioned him deeper into the greenhouse. "Let's find Zeke."

"You know who you're screwing around with?"

"I got a good idea." Rodney waggled the gun again. "Move it."

As they walked through the greenhouse, the misters above them turned on. The cool blast of water felt good on Rodney's skin. At the rear of the building, the country music got louder.

"The growers will be back soon," Jed said.

Rodney didn't believe him, but he said, "Thanks for the warning."

"I'm not sure what you think you're going to get here." Jed glanced over his shoulder. "We're just a bunch of rose farmers."

"Keep moving."

There were two rooms at the back of the greenhouse. The larger one was the office. Its door was open, and Rodney could see inside. A desk and two chairs were all it contained. The smaller room had a placard on the door that read *Restroom/Baño*.

A toilet flushed, and the door opened. A thin man stepped out with a *Guns & Ammo* magazine opened in his hands. He bowed his head as if still reading. He wore a white T-shirt, black shorts, and black tennis shoes. An automatic was on his right hip. "Yo, Jed. You read this article about—?"

Zeke stopped talking when he saw Rodney and Jed.

"The hell is this?" Zeke asked.

"He's robbing us," Jed said.

"The fuck he is." Zeke closed the magazine and put it in his left hand. "You just ended your life, son."

"Take your gun out with your opposite hand," Rodney said.

Zeke's right hand lowered to his holster.

"The other hand." Rodney lifted his gun higher.

"You don't know who you're screwing with."

Rodney wondered why Zeke was making such a big show of it if Booster had called them. He stopped considering the situation when the man yanked his gun from its holster. Rodney squeezed the trigger.

The first bullet hit Zeke squarely in the chest and he

stumbled backward. He continued to bring his gun upward, so Rodney fired again. The second round caught the thin man in the head.

Zeke's skull exploded across the restroom door.

"No!" Jed cried.

Rodney stared at the dead man. Why did he pull his gun? Hadn't Booster called to warn them Rodney was coming?

Jed backpedaled, but Rodney pointed his gun at him. "Stop."

"Whatever you want."

Rodney glanced at Zeke's motionless body. He'd never killed anyone before. It had been surprisingly fast and strangely easy. Rodney kept expecting Zeke to sit up, but the man didn't move. Rodney returned his attention to Jed. "Why'd he go for his gun?"

"Hey, man. What do you want?"

"Where's the money?"

"What money? There ain't no money."

"Quit jerking me around." Rodney jabbed the gun as he spoke. "This isn't a grow operation."

Jed's face pinched. "Look around. What do you think we're doing here?"

"Laundering money."

A new song started. Rodney hadn't heard it before, but the opening lyrics weren't hard to decipher. "Take This Job and Shove It."

The misters shut off and a deeper humidity seemed to settle over the greenhouse.

Jed stared at the body on the floor. "Fine," he said. "You want it? You can have it. The safe's in the office."

Rodney followed him.

A tall safe stood in the far corner. Jed hunched over the

dial as he entered the combination.

"Didn't they tell you I was coming?" Rodney asked.

"Who?" Jed finished entering the combination. He put his hand on the lever and looked at Rodney. "Was this supposed to be an inside job or something? Were Zeke and me supposed to rollover and let you take what's here? Because if we were, we never got told nothing."

Jed turned the handle and opened the door.

Rodney felt sick to his stomach. Why hadn't Booster called? Could something have delayed the man? Maybe the cops stopped him on the way home. Perhaps he'd been arrested. Rodney wanted to give the club president the benefit of the doubt. Otherwise, it meant Booster sent him to rob this place for real.

"Who's operation is this?" Rodney asked.

"You should know. You're ripping it off." Jed motioned toward the open safe. "Didn't you do your homework?"

"Just tell me."

Jed's jaw tightened, and he stayed silent.

Rodney lifted his gun to eye level. "How about I blow off your head?"

"Like you did Zeke's?"

"Tell me whose operation this is, and I'll walk away."

"Without the money? Bullshit." Jed sneered. "Just take it and go already."

Rodney cocked his head. "You're not going to tell me what I want to know?"

"You've signed my death warrant, no matter what happens now. As far as I'm concerned, you can go fuck yourself."

It no longer mattered why Booster sent him to the greenhouse. Rodney couldn't take back what he'd already done. For a felon like him, two murders weren't any worse than one.

So, he fired another round. It was easier the second time.

***

Rodney kept his speed two miles under the limit, and it drove him nuts. He hated driving that way. Cars raced by him. Semis hauling heavy loads passed him. Hell, even a truckload of illegal Mexicans blew past.

But he didn't need to attract the attention of some stupid sheriff.

Rodney caught Highway 28 and drove southwest out of Davenport. That was the highway near the greenhouse. Whoever located the laundering operation there had thought about the need to flee the town in a hurry.

He drove for forty minutes until he entered the small town of Odessa. The whole time, Rodney's heart pounded in his ears. He'd never killed anyone and suddenly he had murdered two men.

Rodney continually wondered what went wrong, but he kept coming back to the same answer—Booster.

The Wasted Souls president sent Rodney to Roses are Red to rob the joint. Either it was a club operation and Booster failed to notify his men to play along, or it was someone else's enterprise and Rodney was supposed to do exactly what he did.

Rodney examined various What If scenarios while driving. He fully believed, if it was a Wasted Souls operation, Booster would have given those men notice. No matter what.

The longer he thought about the What If scenarios, the

angrier Rodney became at himself. How could he have been so stupid? So gullible? He wanted Booster's help, and he believed the man had his best interests at heart.

The Wasted Souls' president was a career criminal, a killer. Rodney should have known better than to trust him. Now Booster had made Rodney exactly like him.

After killing the two men and taking the money, Rodney tried to find the video recording equipment. He spent a few minutes looking but drew a blank. He didn't want to waste too much time in case the growers returned like Jed had said.

Maybe the security cameras were dummies—fakes to convince would-be criminals to stay within the law. Rodney knew businesses did that now and then. Could he have gotten lucky with Roses are Red? After murdering two men, it didn't feel like luck was breaking Rodney's way.

At Odessa, Rodney turned north on Highway 21. It felt as if he were driving all over the state. His panic ebbed some, but Rodney continued to swivel his head, even when he was cruising through open farmland. Rodney occasionally checked the sky for pursuing helicopters.

Why would Booster send him, a lowly prospect, to rob the greenhouse? Was it because the opportunity was there? Rodney needed a job, and Booster found a willing triggerman? Or was it because prospects were expendable? As Booster had said back in Moses Lake, he was as valuable as whale shit.

Had Booster figured out Rodney's secret?

Rodney didn't want to think about that now. Not while running from two murders. He needed to compartmentalize his life. First, he had to put the greenhouse incident behind him.

At the town of Wilbur, Rodney switched to Highway 174, but his panic returned. Even though he'd driven nearly ninety minutes, he'd only gone in a half loop. He was thirty minutes away from Davenport again.

His mouth was dry, and he wanted to stop for a drink. Omak lay ninety minutes to the north.

When he made it to Grand Coulee, Rodney detoured to the state park celebrating the creation of the city's hydroelectricity dam. He parked his truck and got out.

Rodney walked to the edge of the Columbia River and stood below the massive concrete structure. He surreptitiously removed the gun from the back of his pants and clutched it to his belly. Rodney checked for any witnesses. Then he looked a second time just to be sure. Not seeing any, he threw the gun as far as he could into the river.

He returned to his truck and stared at the water.

Rodney gripped the steering wheel when he felt the burning in his eyes. His chest tightened and his chin quivered. Soon, tears ran down his cheeks. He remained in the shadow of the Grand Coulee Dam for twenty minutes, crying for two dead men he wished he'd never met.

6

The Conquering Hero

Rodney drove by the Farm a few minutes before seven. There was no other route for him to get home except to pass by Saxon's place. If any of the Family were standing outside, they'd have seen his truck. Not that it would really matter. Rodney wasn't in trouble with the Old Man.

He'd given Rodney an assignment—pull a job and come back with two grand a piece for the assembled members. He'd accomplished that mission.

However Rodney was sure danger followed him now. Murder put him in a bad mental space, and he couldn't get out of it.

Rodney eyed Saxon's house as his truck sped by. Wiley and Tucker's trucks were missing. Only Kaylee's remained. Saxon's pickup was probably in the garage where he usually kept it.

Hope returned to Rodney when Omak came into view. It was silly to feel hopeful because the town wasn't his home. Spokane was. Or had been most recently. Rodney had bounced around since fleeing Moses Lake in high school. He'd lived all over Eastern Washington including his stints in prison. Kennewick, Yakima, and Spokane. Rodney liked Spokane best because it had the most to do, and also gave him ample opportunities for trouble.

That's how he landed at Coyote Ridge, the state penitentiary in Connell.

Rodney slowly drove through Omak. He should have

felt like the conquering hero who had beaten an enemy and returned home with the spoils of war. Instead, he slunk into town, afraid of the cops and other prying eyes. It was how he had lived most of his life and Rodney hated it, especially now.

He'd robbed the greenhouse to satisfy Saxon's order. Once Rodney brought the money back to the family, the Old Man would have to trust him. Perhaps Saxon would let him into the family. If that happened, the Wasted Souls would patch Rodney in. That was his ultimate goal—to make his life right again.

When he arrived on Main Street, Rodney found a parking spot near his building. He sprung out of the driver's seat and glanced furtively around. Rodney felt naked without his gun. He flipped the bench seat forward and grabbed a small blue bag. It previously held Jed's gym clothes. Now, it held stacks of bills. Rodney returned the seat to its original position and closed the truck door.

Rodney hugged the bag against his body like a running back clutched a football. He hopped onto the sidewalk and continued to search for anyone who appeared threatening. Because of the time, the window installers were gone for the day. The scaffolding had moved down the sidewalk toward the middle of the structure.

If he hurried, Rodney could still grab something to eat at The Saddle Up Diner. They closed at eight.

Rodney trotted up the stairs, unlocked his apartment, and tossed the bag into the hallway. He quickly relocked the door, afraid someone might burst in after him. He felt irrational right now. No one else knew he had ripped off the greenhouse except Booster and Axel.

Rodney wasn't taking any chances.

He leaned a shoulder against the door for several

seconds. Long breaths, in and out of his nose, didn't calm him.

Rodney pushed off the door and snatched the bag. In his bedroom, he dumped the cash onto his bed. The pile of money thrilled him as he set to counting. At first, Rodney didn't believe the number. So he recounted, saying each number aloud as he went. When he finished, he muttered, "Twenty-three thousand. Holy shit."

A small chuckle formed in his throat before it erupted into a full laugh. "I'm rich."

It was the most money he'd ever had in his life. He'd never got to count the money he stole from the bank, let alone spend any of it. The most he ever got from a convenience store was a little over two hundred dollars.

Rodney quickly shoved the cash back into the bag as little giggles bubbled from his throat.

"Twenty-three," he said.

What if he took the money and ran like that old Steve Miller song?

Saxon wouldn't care. He'd chalk it up to Rodney failing to come through on the job.

Booster would know because he'd see the news coming out of Davenport. Still, Rodney was only a prospect.

The cops might make a connection to Rodney. Right now, they didn't know about the Davenport robbery and murders. If he ran, Rodney might give them something to look at. A dot to connect, so to speak. Omak was far enough away from Davenport that maybe it wouldn't matter. Who was he to think he'd even pop up on some detective's radar?

Rodney had a history of theft, and his recent bank robbery certainly elevated his status among the law. His lip curled. It was better to remain in Omak as if nothing had changed. Keep his head down and act normal.

What should I do with the money? Rodney wondered.

He only needed ten thousand to give the Family. That's all Saxon demanded, so that's all the Old Man should get.

A smile spread across Rodney's lips. The rest was his.

"Ten for the Family," he said to himself. "Thirteen for me."

Since that was the case, Rodney could enjoy the fruit of his efforts starting that night. He was tired of living small. He wanted to live like he had deep pockets. Rodney pulled a wad of cash out from the bag and counted two grand.

Besides, if any of the Family saw him, Rodney could always explain he was spending his portion of the take. They'd be none the wiser.

His phone rang, and he pulled it from his pocket. The display screen showed Booster was calling. Had he already heard about the Roses are Red job? Rodney swiped his thumb over the screen to ignore the call. Rodney didn't want to deal with the Wasted Souls' president. Not tonight. He'd talk with Booster tomorrow.

Rodney spread the bills in his hand like he held a royal flush. If he couldn't feel like a conquering hero, perhaps he could feel like something else. Rodney shoved the money into his pocket.

He grabbed the blue bag and tucked it into the closet.

Then he headed for the door. His appetite had returned.

***

"Are you ever gonna get tired of eating these?" Carol slid a Monte Cristo and a side of French fries onto the table.

Rodney pulled the plate closer. "I hope not."

"Anything else?"

"I'm good." He reached for the bottle of ketchup.

"I'll leave you be," she said. "We're gonna start cleaning. Sorry about the noise."

The Saddle Up Diner didn't close for another thirty minutes, but Rodney was the only customer in the restaurant.

He shoved a fry into his mouth as he watched the playback from his security cameras. So far, he hadn't seen any movement in his apartment. Viewing the same stream every night might be boring, but Rodney figured an ounce of prevention was worth a pound of cure.

His grandfather once told him that. It made little sense when he first heard it, but the pithy saying finally rang true.

Some soft country music played in the restaurant. It sounded old by the singer's twang and the simple arrangement of the guitars.

The door to the restaurant opened and Rodney glanced up from the phone. He stopped chewing.

"Well, well, well." Electric Mary tossed her purse onto the booth seat across from him. The woman looked about ready to spill out of her sleeveless black shirt. Her denim shorts rode up high on her thighs and her white sandals revealed recently painted toenails. Bright pink.

Rodney flipped his phone over and pulled it off the table. "Hey."

She leaned over his plate to examine his dinner. Her position gave Rodney a view down her shirt which sent a spike of dopamine through his system. She wasn't wearing a bra. Mary asked, "Didn't you eat that last night?"

"I like consistency."

"Like a married man. That's sweet." Mary slid into the booth.

"What're you doing here?"

"I thought maybe you could take me out. You know? Like on a real date or something."

Carol stopped cleaning a nearby table to look in their direction.

Rodney pointed at his uneaten sandwich. "I just got my dinner."

"I mean after this. Let's go to The Dilly-Dally. Have a few drinks and some laughs. Then we'll go back to your apartment and I'll…" Her words trailed off as if something interrupted her train of thought.

"And you'll what?" Rodney picked up his sandwich.

"Nothing. Did you fix your bed frame?"

"I did."

Her smile was polite. "Maybe we can break it again."

Rodney bit into the Monte Cristo. He shook his head as he chewed.

"What's wrong?" Mary asked.

"I don't wanna go to the tavern."

"Why not?"

Rodney didn't want to run into any of the Family at The Dilly-Dally. "Not in the mood."

"You want to take me someplace nicer?"

He shrugged a single shoulder. "Sure."

"How about the casino?" The 12 Tribes Casino was on the nearby Colville Indian Reservation.

"I don't gamble," Rodney said. "How about the Doghouse?"

Mary rolled her eyes. "You said nice. Let's go to the casino. They got a bar over there. Real fancy. You don't need to gamble or nothing to drink at it."

Rodney bit into his sandwich again. "Maybe," he said through a mouthful.

"Why maybe?"

"Tell me your name."

Her brow furrowed. "Don't be stupid. You already know it."

"You like people calling you Electric Mary?"

She leaned back and her expression hardened. "I don't give you a charge anymore?"

Rodney pretended to be interested in his Monte Cristo. "Well, you wanna hang out tonight. We're supposed to go to the Suicide Race on Saturday. I figure you're trying to make us a thing."

Mary cocked her head. "A thing?"

"Maybe I'm misreading what this is."

The neon Open sign in the window went dark, and the music stopped. Carol spoke with Woody in the kitchen.

Mary's eyes softened. "My name is Mariam Coleman." She looked down at her hands. "Sounds kind of dumb, doesn't it?"

"No," Rodney said. "It doesn't sound dumb. Mariam is real pretty."

"You think we could be a thing?"

He pushed his plate toward her. "Help me eat this, and we'll go to the casino."

***

The casino assaulted Rodney's senses the moment he set foot inside.

Lights flashed on gaming machines. Red bulbs sat atop some like old-school cop cars, hoping to stop wayward gamblers. High-definition screens pulsed with changing colors and imagery.

Digital coins clattered as customers repeatedly tapped

spin buttons. Whirring boops, pulsating beeps, and pleasing squawks accompanied every action on each machine.

Overhead, new wave rock & roll played.

"It's over here," Mary said. She tugged Rodney's hand and led him past a cluster of craps tables.

Two of the tables were empty, but a group of players crowded around the third. A man tossed the dice and yelled, "Hard eight, baby!"

The dealer announced flatly, "Seven, out."

A collective groan rose from the gathered players.

Rodney smiled. He didn't gamble, but he found it fun to watch others do it. He didn't care for the elation when they won, but rather the heartbreaking disappointment when they lost. Rodney had failed plenty in life and it was nice to know it occurred to others, especially when it was by their own hand. He slowed slightly to observe the drama at the craps table, but Mary pulled him along.

"Hey," Rodney said, "let's check this out."

Mary glanced at the table. "Why?"

"Because it's fun."

She slapped his butt. "C'mon. I hate these games."

He shrugged and followed her.

Loggers Pub was tucked in a quieter part of the casino. Mary slid into a booth and encouraged Rodney onto the seat next to her.

"You've really never been here before?" she asked.

He shook his head. "Only been in town a few weeks."

"Most people would find this place right away."

"Casinos aren't my thing." Even as he said that, a cheer erupted from the craps table. He looked back in that direction.

A server walked over. He was a tall, thin man in a dark

shirt and matching slacks. His black hair was braided down his back. "Get you something?"

"Vodka tonic," Mary said.

Rodney nodded once. "The same."

The server walked away.

"What's wrong?" Mary asked.

"Nothing."

Mary bumped his shoulder with hers. "This is way better than The Dilly-Dally, huh?"

Rodney looked at her—*really* looked at her. She had beautiful brown eyes.

"Hey," Mary said. "What's going on? I want to know."

Rodney turned away. He couldn't tell Mary what happened at the greenhouse. No one could ever know.

She squeezed his hand. "You can tell me."

He had to tell her something, so he said, "Tomorrow's my birthday."

"No shit?" Her face brightened. "That's great. Why aren't you happy about that?"

"Makes me think about lost time."

"Fuck that," Mary said. "Let's have a great night, and I'll make your birthday unforgettable." She kissed his neck. "I promise."

The server returned with their drinks and slid them on to the table. "Two vodka tonics," he said. "Anything else?"

"No," Mary said. "Can we start a tab? We're gonna be here for a bit."

He nodded and walked off.

Mary lifted her glass. "To your birthday eve."

Rodney tapped his drink against hers.

"What're we toasting?" A dark-haired woman dropped onto the seat across from them. She carried a glass filled with amber liquid.

Mary stiffened. "What're you doing here?"

"What do you think?" The woman wore a black sweatshirt that read Native Pride. She was attractive with almond-shaped eyes and skin the color of creamed coffee. "Who's this?"

Mary stayed quiet.

The woman slowly blinked, then sipped her drink. "He looks like boyfriend material."

Rodney couldn't tell if the newcomer was sleepy or drunk but went with the latter because of the drink in her hand.

"His name's Rodney," Mary said.

The woman eye's widened as if in recognition. She swirled her drink and opened her mouth to say something, but Mary interrupted her.

"Rodney, this is Dancing Arrow."

The newcomer sniffed. "A real life Indian." Her eyes narrowed. "Ever meet one?"

"Hard not to around here," Rodney said. "I like your name."

Dancing Arrow clucked. "You would."

"Be nice," Mary said.

"Why?" She motioned to Rodney. "They're all the same."

"Not him."

"Whatever." Dancing Arrow sipped from her drink. Her lips pulled back against her teeth as she swallowed.

Mary glared at the newcomer. "Not Rodney. He's not like the others."

Dancing Arrow rolled her eyes, then studied Rodney. "Please accept my apology if I misjudged you."

"It's all right," he said.

"It ain't my real name, anyway. Some jackass named

Wiley slapped me with it in middle school."

Rodney leaned forward. "Wiley Jones?"

"That's the one." Dancing Arrow saluted him with her drink. "He thought it was funny to tease me. Got the whole class in on it, too."

"What's your real name?" Rodney asked.

"Nancy Harrow." She sipped her drink again. "We were talking about Native heritage and lots of others in the class were full-blooded. Know what I mean?"

Rodney glanced around to see if anyone could hear Dancing Arrow since she talked so loudly. She continued unabashed.

"So, I raised my hand to say I was Native, too." Dancing Arrow lifted her hand like she was sitting in class. "Like twenty-five percent Colville on my grandfather's side, but it still counts, especially to white boys." Her eyes went toward the ceiling. "I also got some Vietnamese in me." Dancing Arrow's gaze dropped to Rodney. "That's courtesy of my mom. You ever been with an Asian girl?"

Mary squeezed Rodney's hand. "He's with me."

"Of course he is." Dancing Arrow winked. "They always are."

"Hey," Mary said.

"I'm only teasing." Dancing Arrow swirled her drink. "I was just talking big in front of your boyfriend." She eyed Rodney. "Besides, you know how it is with girls." Her smile was lopsided.

Mary leaned forward. "I said be nice." She squeezed Rodney's hand harder.

Dancing Arrow continued speaking as if she hadn't been admonished. "Anyway, when I said I was twenty-five percent Native, the boys in the class made fun. Wiley was the worst. He started with the Dancing Arrow bullshit and the others joined in. After a while, I stopped fighting it."

"Want me to call you Nancy?" Rodney asked.

"You're sweet." Nancy's smile grew more lopsided. "But no, not around here. I've been Dancing Arrow so long only the Social Security office knows me as Nancy."

Rodney sipped his drink. "So, how do you know each other?"

"Small town," they said in unison. Neither woman found it a funny coincidence.

Overhead, a new song started. It was the one about every girl being crazy about a sharp-dressed man. Rodney was dressed in jeans and a black T-shirt. He couldn't imagine any girl going for him dressed the way he was.

Dancing Arrow leaned to the side and reached into her pocket. When she straightened, she popped something into her mouth. She washed it down with her drink.

"What was that?" Mary asked.

"A pick-me-up. Want one?"

"Not tonight."

Dancing Arrow's gaze shifted to Rodney. "What about you?"

Rodney shook his head.

"Just me, I guess. Ticket for one." Dancing Arrow slowly spun her glass on the table. "What were you toasting when I showed up?"

"Nothing," Mary said. Her eyes hardened when she looked at Rodney. "We were just kicking off the night."

"Then let's do it right." Dancing Arrow slipped out of the booth and headed toward the bar.

"Who is she?" Rodney asked.

"A friend."

"She doesn't seem like it."

Mary watched Dancing Arrow talk with the bartender.

"We've got some history."

"What kind?"

"It's not important."

Rodney slid toward the edge of the booth. "Let's ditch her and go back to my place."

Mary grabbed his arm. "Let's stay here."

He cocked his head. "Even with her being in our business?"

"Just a couple drinks, then we'll go."

Rodney slid closer and put his arm around her shoulders. "You sure everything's okay?"

Mary forced a smile. "Everything's great. Why wouldn't it be?"

Dancing Arrow walked over with three shot glasses. She carefully sat before placing the small glasses on the table in front of both Mary and Rodney. Dancing Arrow held hers out for a toast.

"What is it?" Mary asked.

"Fireball."

Cinnamon whiskey, thought Rodney. Alcohol for teenagers. He grabbed the shot and lifted it.

Mary did the same.

The three clinked their glasses together.

"To friends," Dancing Arrow said before tossing it back.

"To friends," Mary muttered unenthusiastically.

Rodney drank the hot whiskey in a single swallow. To friends, he thought.

7

The Perfect Girl

Rodney McCready woke to sunlight on his face. His head pounded and a wave of nausea ran through him. He rolled over to throw up and bumped into Mary. She lay there sleeping.

He pushed himself upright and discovered he wasn't in his apartment. Rodney was in a hotel room, a nice clean one with modern amenities. It didn't take him long to surmise he was still in the casino.

Sickness rushed through him again. Rodney tossed the sheet off and padded hurriedly toward the bathroom. He closed the door with a bang. He dropped to his knees as his stomach revolted.

Rodney clutched the edge of the toilet and heaved. His body attempted to give back everything he'd put into it the night before. All the alcohol. The Monte Cristo and the French fries, too. Tears welled in his eyes as his stomach twisted and squeezed.

When he finished, Rodney flushed the toilet. His head thumped as he lay on the cold bathroom tile.

He closed his eyes as images of the previous evening drifted back to him.

One shot led to a second. He remembered dancing and laughing with Mary. Or was it with Dancing Arrow? He definitely danced with both women. Why would Mary allow that to happen? She seemed so protective of him at the beginning of their night.

How many drinks had they had? Rodney had no recollection. Usually when he drank, he could remember how much alcohol he consumed. *Usually*, he was very careful in that regard, and more recently, downright obsessive about it.

The cold floor felt good on the side of his face. A memory came to him then. Mary and Dancing Arrow kissing at their table, and the bartender telling them to get a room.

Rodney opened his eyes and pushed off the floor. His head banged harder, and he thought he might vomit a second time.

He opened the bathroom door.

Mary sat on the edge of the bed with the sheet wrapped around her. She held her head in her hands. "Where are we?" she muttered through her fingers. She didn't look up.

"This must've been your friend's room."

Rodney found his underwear and slipped them on.

Mary lifted her head. "What're you doing?"

"What's it look like?" His tone was sharp.

"It looks like you're leaving."

"No flies on you."

Her brow furrowed. "What's that mean?"

Rodney grabbed his pants. "It means you're quick."

Mary stood. "Are you blaming me for something?"

He shoved his hands into the front pockets of his pants. His heart sank. He checked the other remaining pockets, then lowered his pants in despair. "She took my money."

"What's that?"

"Your fucking friend." Rodney lifted his pants and angrily shook them. "She stole my two thousand."

Mary stared at him. "You had two grand?"

He slapped his jeans against the ground. "Goddamn it."

"I didn't have anything to do with this."

Rodney jammed a leg into his jeans. "She's your friend."

"It looks like we both slept with her."

"Probably not your first time."

Her face tightened. "What's that supposed to mean?"

Rodney slipped his second leg into the jeans. "I don't know."

"Why're you mad at me?"

He tugged the pants into place. "Do you remember what happened last night?"

"Not really."

"Goddamn it," he muttered again.

"Stop being mad at me."

"She roofied us."

"It wasn't a roofie."

Rodney glared at her. "Then what was it?"

"Probably X."

"Ecstasy?" He stared at Mary. "Are you for real?"

"Most guys would be happy they had sex with two women."

Rodney's jaw dropped. "You planned this?"

She shook her head. "No way. I didn't want any of it, but I'm trying to look on the bright side—for you."

Rodney threw his hands in the air. "There's no bright side. I'm out two grand."

"Fine." Mary held up a defiant hand. "Don't take it out on me."

"Did I say anything last night?"

Her eyes narrowed. "Like what?"

"I don't know." He turned around. Rodney couldn't come out and ask Mary what he really wanted to. He had to be cryptic. "Did I say any weird shit?"

"I don't remember. I don't even remember the sex."

Rodney grabbed his T-shirt and pulled it over his head.

Mary hopped onto the bed and kneeled. She kept the sheet around her by tucking it into her armpits. "Please don't go. It's your birthday."

He held up his hand. Rodney had to get out of the room and do some thinking. He'd been very careful with his drinking since leaving prison. If he ever said the wrong thing to anyone, he could wind up dead.

"I need to be alone," Rodney said.

"I thought you liked me." Mary reached for him, but he pulled away. "Are you upset because of the three-way? It's not that big of a deal. I promise."

Rodney cocked his head. "You've done it before?"

"Only because the guys liked it."

His lip curled. "Not me."

"What's changed?" Mary asked. She waved her hands as if dismissing her question. "We won't do it ever again. I promise."

"Whatever." Rodney searched for his shoes and socks.

"Please, I'll be the perfect girl for you. Whatever you want, Rodney, let me be that woman for you."

He dropped onto the floor and slipped his socks and shoes on. "Stop talking."

Mary hovered above him on the bed. "I'll do anything for you."

"You don't even know me."

"I know it's your birthday."

Rodney fumbled with his laces. He wanted to get out of the hotel room to clear his head. Worries about saying something wrong to Dancing Arrow plagued him. He could barely think about anything else.

"Let's run away," Mary said. "We'll go someplace far

from here and never come back."

Rodney stood. "Where does she live?"

"Who? Nancy? Why do you want to know?"

"I want to talk with her."

Suspicion flooded Mary's eyes. "You want to see her again."

Rodney flicked his hand at Mary. "Get out of here with that bullshit." He couldn't go into the reasons for speaking with Dancing Arrow. Frustration overwhelmed him. "I don't have time for your craziness."

Mary jumped off the bed, leaving the sheet behind. She stood in front of him, naked.

"Please, don't go back to your apartment." She reached for his hands, but Rodney pushed her away.

"Stop!"

"I'll be perfect," Mary said in a small voice. She kept her arms by her sides. "Just tell me how you want me to be."

"It's too late."

Rodney stepped out of the hotel room and hurried down the hallway.

***

Rodney angrily swung the apartment door closed after entering. It banged against the frame but failed to close. He swore, returned to the door, and shut it.

He peeled off his clothing as he walked to the bathroom.

Rodney fumed the entire drive home. It wasn't far from the casino, only a few minutes, so he wasn't able to shake his anger at Dancing Arrow.

"The bitch," he yelled. "The goddamn bitch!"

He pulled the shower curtain back and started the water.

It ran cold. While the water heated, Rodney stared at his reflection in the mirror. "You're a dumb ass." His jaw tightened. He could continue to hurl terrible insults at himself but what would it accomplish?

Dancing Arrow had slipped him a drug, and he'd blacked out most of the night. When she woke up, Nancy had stolen the cash he had in his pocket. Worse than that, he might have said something to her and compromised everything the Wasted Souls expected him to do. So much depended on him getting accepted into the Family.

Rodney stepped into the shower and hurriedly cleaned himself. Worst-case scenarios ran through his head.

What if he told Dancing Arrow about the two men he killed at the greenhouse? Rodney pulled the job for Saxon and the Family. It was a small town. Perhaps Rodney mentioned a name she recognized.

Or maybe he told Dancing Arrow about the Wasted Souls. Rodney was careful to hold his tongue around anyone. However, if he had too much to drink, those barriers he kept always became tenuous.

Rodney's current life was built on misdirection, untruths, and tenuous connections. The lies started before he ever approached the motorcycle club—a move made possible by his relationship with his cousin. The link to Saxon Peckham's Family happened when Rodney casually mentioned his former cellmate's interesting backstory to Booster and Axel. Had he known the turn of events it would lead to, Rodney would have kept his mouth shut.

Like he should have done last night.

He stopped the shower and dried off with a musty smelling towel. Rodney dressed in a clean T-shirt he pulled out of the dresser. He wore the same pair of jeans he had on earlier. After he put on his tennis shoes, he was ready to see the Family.

Rodney opened the closet doors and stared at the empty floor where the bag of money should have been.

"What the fuck?"

***

"What're you having?" Carol asked. She held her notebook and pen at the ready.

Rodney looked up from his cell phone. He'd just started Intruder Defender Plus, the security camera app. "Coffee," he said, "and some eggs."

"That's it?"

He frowned. The hangover pounded inside his skull. The last thing he wanted to do was screw around with a breakfast order. "I don't know. Some toast, too."

"Geez," Carol said. "Don't bite my head off about it." She turned and walked away.

Rodney started to say he was sorry, but a table full of regulars glared at him.

He returned his attention to the phone.

Before coming down to The Saddle Up Diner, Rodney ran through his apartment. Nothing else was missing. There really wasn't anything to steal, though. He didn't have anything of value, except the bag of money hidden in his closet.

So how did anyone know it was there? If someone saw him leave his truck with it, they'd only think he had a bag of gym clothes. No one in their right mind would assume it was full of cash.

Rodney started the video playback from the bedroom camera. He set the time from when he left the apartment the previous evening. The money was in the closet then. He played it back at eight times the normal speed, but it looked as if nothing moved. It was like watching grass grow, only more boring.

Had someone followed him from the greenhouse in Davenport? Rodney was sure no one had. He kept a watchful eye out for any tails. When he stopped in Grand Coulee to throw the gun into the river, Rodney would have surely spotted someone following him then.

Someone found out about the money after he got home. So, how?

Dancing Arrow.

Rodney must have talked about the money after she drugged him. He grimaced and fought back the expletive he wanted to shout.

Carol brought him a cup of coffee. "Hope this helps your attitude."

Rodney paused the playback and turned the phone over. "I'm sorry."

"Rough morning?"

"You could say that."

She smiled. "Maybe it'll get better."

He didn't know what to say to that, so he said, "It's my birthday."

"You don't look happy about it."

He shrugged.

"Then I won't sing to you."

Carol moved on to some other customers, and Rodney restarted the video. Nothing moved in the frame, and he needed to watch the time clock to ensure it was actually playing.

Rodney's thoughts returned to Dancing Arrow. If he told her about the money, he must have told her about the robbery. After she slipped him the drug, Dancing Arrow probably stole his keys, entered his apartment, and took the bag of money.

"Yeah," he mumbled. "That's how it played out."

Except his keys were in his jeans when he woke up. Rodney's lips tightened.

So, Dancing Arrow swiped the cash and keys from his pockets, then went to his apartment where she stole the bag of money. Afterward, she returned to the hotel room and slipped the keys back into his jeans.

That didn't seem right.

Rodney hunched over the phone when there was some movement on the screen. He slowed the playback speed to normal.

"No fucking way," he muttered.

On the video, Tucker Skillingstad and Kaylee Zavala entered Rodney's bedroom. Were other family members in his apartment, too? Rodney didn't have to wonder how they got in.

His keys always hung on the wall hook whenever he was at the Farm. Someone must have duplicated the key. Either they did it at the house or they took his keys to a hardware store during the times Rodney accompanied Tucker or Wiley on their errands.

Tucker and Kaylee glanced around the bedroom as if they were unsure what they should search for. Tucker dropped to his hands and knees to look under the bed—there wasn't anything under there.

Kaylee checked the closet and found the small gym bag. Tucker stood and moved to the dresser but before he could open a drawer, she said something. Tucker looked at her and Kaylee spread the gym bag open. The two hurried out of the bedroom.

Carol returned to his table then. "Here you go. Eggs and toast."

Rodney forced a smile. "Thank you."

"Holler if you need anything."

There was no way anyone in the Family knew he had the money. He hadn't called Saxon to say the job was through. He wanted to show up unannounced at the Farm and drop the bag.

Rodney absently buttered the first piece of toast. No one knew about the money unless he mentioned something to Dancing Arrow. In that case, why didn't she take his keys and steal the money?

Mary, Rodney thought. He quickly dismissed the concern. She stayed with him all night.

Rodney bit into the toast and remembered Mary's last words. "Don't go back to your apartment." Actually, those weren't her last words. She said she'd be his perfect girl. Why didn't she want him to go back to his apartment?

Because she knew something bad had happened. Or something was going to happen. Whatever it was, Mary seemed hesitant for either of them to go back to the apartment.

Had Mary lied about being drugged like him? Was she involved with the Family? Booster had warned him about the Family being bigger than Rodney suspected. Maybe Rodney talked about the greenhouse robbery last night and Mary called Tucker or Kaylee.

Rodney didn't think so. Mary looked as rough as he felt and she was mad at Dancing Arrow for drugging her, too. Then why didn't she want Rodney to go back to his apartment? What did she know?

He shoved the last bite of toast into his mouth.

His thoughts returned to the night Mary was in his

house. It was the only time they'd been there. She'd been with him the entire time, except…

Rodney grabbed his phone and started the security app again. The camera footage only stayed for three days, then it deleted itself. He was on the Bronze plan. If he marked footage to keep, the system would archive it forever. However, there was only so much storage in his plan. If he paid for the Premium service, the unarchived footage would remain for two weeks. That was excessive, though.

He called up the night Mary visited and played the video at eight times its normal speed. As the video raced along, they shed their clothes and hopped onto his bed. Rodney looked up, worried someone might notice his homemade pornography. He hid the screen with both hands.

Even though it was him and Mary having sex, it was like watching a strange comedy. The sped-up action made it seem awkward and, at times, flailing. After the bed broke, they rolled off to the floor. The two hurried to the living room.

Rodney paused the video and noted the time. He selected the living room camera at the desired time. He and Mary continued their coupling on the couch. When they finished, they sat together. Mary got up and disappeared.

It required him to switch between the cameras in the hallway and the bedroom. Mary exited the bathroom, dug in her purse. She looked up and said something. That's when Rodney asked what she was doing and she said, "Grabbing my purse."

Mary entered his bedroom and put something behind the nightstand. When she returned to the living room, she carried a can of beer in her left hand. Her right hand was cupped. She scooted the coffee table closer to them with the right hand.

"Goddamn it," Rodney muttered.

He paused the video and shoved the phone into his pocket. Rodney waved to Carol. "I'll take the check now."

***

Rodney entered his apartment in a quiet and controlled manner. He walked into his bedroom and went directly for the nightstand. He leaned over and found a small round disc stuck to its backside.

It wasn't a camera—not with where Mary put it.

He reached for it and paused. Now he knew it was there, what danger was it? Better to let the Family think they still had a leg up on him.

This was how they knew he had the money, but what had they heard? A closet door opening and closing?

No, Rodney thought. They heard him counting the money. They heard the final tally. Rodney lowered his head. They heard him bragging to himself.

"Dumb ass," he muttered.

The Family must have figured he had gotten some cash. They probably reckoned he pulled a job somewhere. Why had they taken the money before he'd given it to them?

Because Saxon told Rodney he had to pull a job netting ten grand. He'd done one where the proceeds were more than double that. Rodney had planned not to share everything with the Family. They just made sure he was going to be honest.

He held back an expletive.

So Mary was definitely working with the Family. At least, she hadn't planted the microphone before they had sex.

Rodney went to the living room next and checked underneath the coffee table. A second small disc was stuck there. Mary had encouraged him into another round of coupling so the Family could hear them. Why did she do that? Was it to prove something to the others?

He clenched his fists and fought back the desire to shout at Saxon and his cronies.

A thought occurred to him. Why did they even need Mary to plant the microphones?

If Saxon had a copy of his key, someone could have come into his apartment whenever they wanted to plant the bugging devices.

Were they testing Mary, too? If that was the case, why?

Maybe someone had already planted bugs in his apartment. Perhaps those weren't simply listening devices and were cameras like the ones he installed.

Rodney sat on his couch and thought. If that was true, what had he said or done inside his apartment that he didn't want anyone to know about?

He'd been careful to say nothing. Rodney always behaved as if people might be listening—a trait developed in prison. If the Family heard his phone call to Booster yesterday morning, they wouldn't learn anything except Rodney called a friend for help.

If they had planted cameras in his apartment, the only thing inappropriate they might have seen was him masturbating in the shower.

Rodney's phone rang. He removed it from his pocket. The caller ID screen showed it was Tucker.

He steeled himself before answering. "Hello?"

"Where you at?" Tucker asked.

"My apartment." Rodney thought about adding, "as if you didn't know," but he kept it to himself.

"Saxon wants you out at the Farm."

"All right."

"And, hey."

"Yeah?"

"If you see Wiley, steer clear of him. He's really pissed at you."

"What for?" Rodney asked, even though he knew why.

"C'mon, man," Tucker said. "It's a small town."

Wiley had probably heard them having sex. Rodney straightened. He remembered Mary saying clearly Wiley would never have another shot with her.

Rodney grinned. The microphones didn't seem so bad right then.

Liar, Liar, Pants on Fire

"Well," Saxon Peckham said. "How'd you do?" The Old Man flicked his cigarette into the gravel driveway. He was dressed in his customary overalls and dingy white T-shirt.

"I failed," Rodney said.

Wiley stood to Saxon's left. His cheeks flushed as he glared at Rodney. He balled his hands and hunched his shoulders. His cowboy hat was pulled low on his forehead. Wiley shifted his weight as if itching to jump forward and hit Rodney.

Kaylee and Tucker waited to the Old Man's right. They both wore masks of innocence. Neither seemed bothered by breaking into Rodney's apartment and stealing the bag of money.

Nolan leaned on the porch railing, sipping a beer.

"You know what failure means?" Saxon asked.

Rodney nodded. "I do."

The Old Man rocked back and forth on his heels and toes. "You ain't got no excuse?"

"I couldn't get it done."

Wiley blurted, "Let's stop screwing around with him."

Saxon cast a sideways glance. "Easy."

"We know—"

The Old Man faced Wiley now. "Hold your blasted tongue or go inside."

"I don't have to take your shit, Saxon."

Nolan straightened. "Watch it."

Wiley pointed at the Canadian. "Stay up there!"

Tucker moved closer to the Old Man.

"You, too!" Wiley stepped back. His features contorted with rage. "I see what you're all doing!"

"What're we doing?" Saxon asked.

"Choosing him over me." Wiley motioned to Rodney. "That's why you sent her—"

"Inside!" Saxon barked.

Wiley shuffled back and raised his hands. "You're picking him."

The Old Man thumbed toward the house. "Now."

"Whatever."

"We'll talk about this later."

Wiley slowly moved toward the stairs.

Saxon faced Rodney. "There's a report out of Davenport. Someone shot up a greenhouse. Couple men killed. Know anything about that?"

Wiley ascended the stairs to the porch. He glanced back at Rodney, waiting to hear the answer to the Old Man's question.

Rodney shook his head. He didn't like the tone in Saxon's voice or the way the Family members watched him. Playing dumb seemed the right course of action. "What's there to steal from a greenhouse?"

Nolan sipped his beer as he leaned on the porch railing. It seemed as if he were studying Rodney.

Tucker crossed his arms and narrowed his eyes. It was the same look Rodney had seen during their days in Coyote Ridge. He did that when he was unsure of himself.

Kaylee looked down at her feet. She nudged a pebble with the toe of her shoe.

"We got a problem," Saxon said. He shoved his hands

into the pockets of his overalls and returned to rocking on his heels and toes.

"What's that?"

Wiley paused on the porch. He stood with his hand on the screen door, but continued to watch the interaction between Rodney and the Old Man.

"You're lying," Saxon said.

Rodney stayed quiet.

Wiley smiled. "Liar, liar, pants on fire."

The Old Man spun and pointed a crooked finger at him. "What'd I tell you?"

"Goddamn it." Wiley jerked the door open and stepped inside.

"Why didn't you make sure he went in?" Saxon asked Nolan.

The Canadian shrugged. "He's my responsibility?"

"We're all our brothers' keeper." The Old Man glanced at Tucker and Kaylee. "Remember that."

They nodded in unison.

Saxon turned around. "Growing is never easy."

"No, sir," Rodney said.

"Tell the truth now."

What truth did Saxon want? Rodney had told so many lies he no longer knew exactly where the truth started. So, he said the only thing he could. "I failed to do the job."

Saxon inhaled deeply and held his breath. After a moment, he exhaled. "You lie not to make an excuse, not to rationalize the situation."

Rodney furrowed his brow.

"I appreciate that." The Old Man waved his arm at the others. "We appreciate that."

Nolan tipped his beer. Tucker stared at Rodney. Kaylee continued to look down at her feet.

"You didn't fail," Saxon said. "Did you?"

Rodney shook his head once.

"You had the money." The Old Man closed his mouth and struggled to contain those big teeth of his. "What I want to know is how you got it."

"How'd you know I didn't fail?" Rodney asked. "How'd you know about the money?"

Saxon rubbed his chin. "How do you think? We stole it from you."

Kaylee looked up, but Rodney's face remained expressionless.

"That doesn't surprise you?" Saxon asked.

"I figured it was someone in the Family." Rodney glanced at Tucker, then Kaylee. "But how'd you know about the money? Why'd you take it when you were going to get your cut?"

Saxon waved the questions away. "Worries for another day. The only question that matters is, where did the money come from?"

Rodney flexed his jaw and remained silent.

"Well?"

"Why's it matter?" Rodney asked. "You gave me a job, and I did it. I held to my end of the bargain, then you broke into my apartment and stole from me. It seems you're the one who has questions to answer for."

The Old Man glanced back at Nolan. The Canadian put his beer on the railing and came down the stairs.

Rodney lifted his hands. "Hey, now."

Tucker stepped forward. "C'mon, Rodney. Don't make this harder than it has to be."

Kaylee moved out of the way.

Rodney still had his truck keys in his pocket. When he arrived, the Family came out to him, so he didn't hang them on the wall. He could never make it to his pickup before Nolan and Tucker could grab him.

"Either start talking," Saxon said, "or we'll make you talk."

"Fine." Rodney held out his hands as he backpedaled toward his truck. "Just stay where you are."

Nolan and Tucker kept approaching.

"I said stop." Rodney pointed at both men.

"You're not dictating the situation," Saxon said. "Where'd you get the money?"

"The greenhouse," Rodney shouted. "I got it from the fucking greenhouse! All right?"

Nolan and Tucker each grabbed an arm. Their fingers dug into Rodney's skin. He tried to pull free, but it was like they caught him in dual vises.

Saxon said, "That's disappointing."

"What'd I do?" Rodney glanced at Tucker and Nolan. "What'd I do?"

"That greenhouse," Saxon said, "belongs to a client. You might have seen their representative."

"The guy in the Lexus?" Panic laced Rodney's words.

The Old Man asked, "How'd you know about the greenhouse?"

"A friend, but I didn't know it was linked to the Family."

Nolan and Tucker jostled him back and forth.

"What's this friend's name?" Saxon asked.

"I can't tell you."

Saxon sighed. "I thought you might say that." He turned to Kaylee. "Go get Wiley."

"Wait," Rodney said.

"The time for waiting is over." The Old Man lifted his chin toward the barn. "Tie him up."

Rodney fought to get free as Nolan and Tucker dragged him away.

***

Wiley slugged Rodney in the head and the chair fell over.

"Pow," Wiley said with a laugh. "Conor McGregor returns to the ring."

Rodney's face lay in the dirt. The aroma of cat urine was stronger on the ground. His hands and ankles were bound with duct tape to one of the kitchen chairs he'd tossed onto the debris pile only days before. He wondered if others had experienced the same fate he did now.

"I'll tell you what you want to know," Rodney croaked.

"In a minute," Saxon said. "You need to be in the right state of mind."

Wiley danced around and jabbed at the air. "I could do this all day."

Nolan and Tucker lifted Rodney back into his sitting position.

"Don't you think he's had enough?" Kaylee asked.

Wiley spun and stuck a finger in her face. "I'll say when he's had enough."

"No," the Old Man said. "I say when." The four of them stared at Saxon. "He's not had even close to enough."

Wiley jumped next to the chair and punched Rodney on the right side of the head. He immediately twisted his hips and cracked Rodney on the left temple.

Rodney slumped as darkness crept in from the edges of his consciousness.

***

Rodney came to when water splashed him in the face. His entire body was wet.

Tucker stood in front of him with a metal bucket. Regret filled his eyes.

"Ready to talk now?" Saxon asked from a corner of the barn.

"I was ready before we came in here."

"Eh." The Old Man waggled a hand. "That's debatable."

Wiley stood nearby, rubbing his knuckles. The man seemed beside himself with glee.

Nolan and Kaylee huddled off to the side. It didn't take a psychologist to see neither of them wanted to be in the barn.

Rodney spat blood on the ground next to his chair. "I robbed the greenhouse."

"We've established that," Saxon said. He came closer now and pushed Tucker out of the way. "How'd you learn about it?"

"A friend."

"Let me hit him again," Wiley said. He threw a jab-cross combination in the air. "He'll shit the truth sooner or later."

The Old Man held up his hand. "You've loosened enough truth. Isn't that right, Rodney?"

He nodded.

"Who is this friend?"

"Henry Wade," Rodney lied.

Henry was truly Rodney's old friend, but they hadn't talked since Rodney left Moses Lake as a boy.

"How'd this Henry fella know about the greenhouse?"

"He heard a rumor." The lie continued to flow. Rodney

was building the story in his head, trying to answer the questions he thought Saxon would ask.

"A rumor?" Saxon's face hardened. "I'm supposed to believe you hit the greenhouse on a rumor?"

"He said the greenhouse was a cover for a drug operation."

"Drugs?" the old man asked.

"He said there were always Mexicans coming and going."

Saxon hunched closer to Rodney. "What's a bunch of beaners got to do with it?"

"Bullshit," Wiley said. "He's lying."

The Old Man waved a hand for Wiley to be quiet. "Answer the question."

Rodney said, "Henry's got a nose for these things."

"He a cop or something?"

"He used to be." Rodney figured if he told Saxon his make-believe contact was a policeman, the Old Man would either want to meet him or he'd decide to never trust Rodney. "He got busted for taking money."

Saxon stared at Rodney for several seconds.

"You're not really believing this story?" Wiley said. "Beaners and a dirty cop? It's bullshit."

Rodney eyed Wiley. "If it's bullshit, tell me how I learned about it. Huh?"

"I wanna meet this former policeman," Saxon said.

"Yeah," Rodney said, fighting back a sigh of relief. "No problem."

"Did he hit the greenhouse with you?"

"I did the job myself."

Wiley threw his hands in the air. "Now, I know he's full of shit. No way this pussy killed two guys. Look at him."

"I shot the first one when he came out of the john,"

Rodney said. "He wouldn't listen."

Tucker's eyes widened. He seemed shocked at Rodney's admission.

"And the second?" Saxon asked.

"I shot him in the office after he opened the safe."

"Why?"

"Because after I killed the first guy, the second didn't matter."

"Oh my God," Wiley said. "You all can't believe this."

Kaylee shuffled toward the opening of the barn, but she didn't leave. Nolan remained in the shadows.

Saxon rubbed his chin. "Christ. You created a mess."

"I didn't know there were places I couldn't hit."

The Old Man's expression darkened. "Don't put this on me."

"I'm not." Rodney's shoulders hurt from being pinched behind his back. "Whose money did I take?"

Saxon's eyelids drooped as he studied Rodney. Several moments passed. Rodney became acutely aware of the sounds around him. The sporadic traffic on the highway. A feral cat yowling outside the barn. Kaylee absently kicking at pebbles.

"Ever hear of the Savage Renegades?" Saxon finally asked.

"Seriously?" Rodney said. "Everyone's heard of them."

The Renegades were a west side organization with chapters from Bellingham, Washington, to Eureka, California. They even had chapters in British Columbia. According to Booster, the Wasted Souls and Renegades had once been friendly clubs, but that ended in the '90s during a shootout in Las Vegas.

"Who was the guy in the Lexus?" Rodney asked.

"Their attorney," Saxon said.

"What was he doing here?"

"If you keep asking questions, I'm going to have Wiley adjust your attitude again."

Rodney bowed his head.

Saxon put his hand on Rodney's shoulder. "Word is twenty-three thousand is missing from the greenhouse. We only found twenty-one in your apartment. What happened to the rest?"

"I took it to the casino."

"Go on a losing streak?" The Old Man leaned in. "Before you lie, I already know the truth."

Rodney eyed Saxon. Maybe he knew the truth, maybe he didn't. Perhaps Mary already told him about their night. This was Rodney's opportunity to blend some truth in with his story.

"I was with a couple of girls," he said.

"What're their names?"

"Electric Mary and Dancing Arrow."

Kaylee clucked her tongue. "Sluts."

"Hey," Wiley snapped. "You're no better."

"I'll fucking stab you." Kaylee moved quickly across the barn. Nolan moved to intercept her.

Wiley grinned. "Bring it on."

"What happened to the money?" Saxon asked.

"Dancing Arrow stole it."

"She stole it?" This obviously surprised the Old Man.

Kaylee stopped to listen. Nolan's arm remained wrapped around her waist.

"I woke up in the morning," Rodney said. "Dancing Arrow was gone along with my cut." Rodney's gaze cut to Wiley. "Only Mary remained in my bed."

"You son of a bitch." Wiley jumped at him.

Saxon shouted, "Control yourself!"

Tucker grabbed Wiley under the armpits and pulled him back.

"He's trying to wind you up," the Old Man said.

"Let him!" Wiley shouted over his shoulder. "I'll bust him another one." Tucker pushed him out of the barn.

"Sluts!" Kaylee yelled after him.

Saxon turned back to Rodney. "If the Renegades get a whiff you were involved with the greenhouse, I'm serving you up. You haven't made yourself indispensable yet."

"I understand."

Saxon's lips twisted with anger. "Keep your mouth shut. Don't tell anyone. Understand?"

Rodney nodded.

"You put the Family in a bad situation." Saxon turned to Nolan. "Untie him and clean him up." He left the barn.

Nolan hurried over and squatted next to the chair. He cut the tape securing Rodney's right arm. "Man, I'm sorry you had to go through that."

"It's all right," Rodney said. "I did it to myself."

Kaylee walked over. "You okay?"

"I've been better."

"We've all been in the chair," Nolan said, "at one time or another."

Kaylee crossed her arms. "The chair sucks."

Rodney's arm popped free. "Jesus, I thought I was going to die in that chair today."

She frowned. "We had the same thought."

He eyed her but didn't ask what he was thinking. Did the Family members think they would die when it was their time in the chair? Or did they think Rodney was going to die today?

9

Blast from the Past

Rodney washed his face in the bathroom sink. Bloody water swirled around the basin before it disappeared down the drain. He ran his tongue around his teeth; none were broken. The inside of his mouth felt like hamburger, though.

He splashed more cold water on his cheeks and gingerly touched them again. If he were home, he would have fashioned an icepack to hold against them. Doing so at the Farm would look weak. Rodney would never give Wiley the satisfaction.

Outside, a loud engine approached. Rodney stepped to the window and moved the curtain. A silver and red pickup bounced down the driveway. He'd never seen it before. Rodney let the fabric fall back into place.

He turned off the water and studied his wet face in the mirror. Wiley had hit him multiple times but never punched him directly in the eyes or the nose. His cheeks were red, and the skin was torn in several places. Dribbles of blood continued to leak out from the cuts. Rodney didn't have a broken nose and his eyes weren't blackened. He should count himself lucky.

A metallic squeak occurred beyond the window, followed by a quick *thunk*. Footsteps moved through the house before muffled voices started outside. Soon, laughter mixed with the conversation.

Rodney gently dried his face with a hand towel. Spots

of blood lingered on the white cloth. He tossed it into the hamper before leaving the bathroom.

He walked through the house and paused long enough to hear voices drifting from the living room. Some of the Family lingered around the television. It sounded like *Judge Judy* was on again.

Rodney wanted to know who arrived at the Farm, so he quietly headed outside.

Tucker stood near the hood of a mid-'80s GMC truck and laughed with the driver, a smaller man in blue jeans and a curled brim baseball hat. When he noticed Rodney approaching, Tucker said, "Hey, let me introduce you to my friend—"

The driver turned, and his eyes widened. "Rodney McCready?"

"Bobby Tobeck?"

"Holy shit," the driver said with a laugh. "How the hell are you?"

Rodney stuck out his hand. "I'm good."

Bobby grabbed his hand and pulled him in for a bro hug, the embrace men used to simulate intimacy everywhere except prison. When they parted, Bobby asked, "What happened to your face?"

"I fell down."

Disbelief filled Bobby's eyes, but he said, "I understand. I've fallen before."

Tucker put his hand on Rodney's shoulder. "How do you two know each other?"

"High school," Bobby said.

Rodney shook his head. "You were in school. I was just bumming around, looking for trouble."

"You found it if I remember correct."

"Yeah." Rodney's gaze cut to Tucker. "I hung around

with Bobby and his friends until I got caught trying to steal some CDs. Went to juvenile hall. My dad drove all the way from Moses Lake to pick me up. Didn't set me on the straight and narrow, though. I took off the next day and went back to Spokane."

"I didn't see you for like five years after that." Now, Bobby eyed Tucker. "Next time we saw each other was at this shitty bar in the valley." He turned to Rodney. "What was its name?"

"Bottoms Up or something like that."

Bobby snapped his fingers. "That's the one. What a night, huh?"

"Hey, whatever happened to that girl you were chasing?"

"She let me take her out a couple nights before she dumped me for some dude with a bike."

"Like in a motorcycle gang?" Rodney wondered if it might have been a member of the Wasted Souls.

Bobby laughed. "No. Like those idiots pretending they're racing the Tour de France every weekend."

Tucker lightly smacked Bobby on the arm. "Listen, I'll go get Saxon and let you two catch up." He smiled at both men before bounding into the house.

Rodney watched Tucker go. When the screen door closed, Rodney turned back to the new arrival and moved in closer.

"Man," Bobby said, "blast from the past, huh?"

Rodney waved off his comment. He whispered, "You gotta leave."

"What're you talking about?"

"Leave now. Don't ask questions. Just do it."

Confusion crossed Bobby's face. "Tell me why."

"Remember how you tried to look out for me, but I

didn't listen and ended up in juvie? This is me returning the favor."

Bobby motioned toward the house. "I've worked with these guys before."

"Meet me tonight at the Doghouse and I'll tell you everything. Whatever they want you to do, you've gotta say no. Trust me."

The screen door opened, and Tucker stepped outside.

Wiley followed closely behind. He had changed his clothes. He now wore a faded Black Sabbath T-shirt, blue jeans, and the stupid straw cowboy hat.

"Back Road Bobby," Wiley said cheerfully. When he noticed Rodney standing so close to the new arrival, he added, "Move away from him, baby bird. He's no one you need to know."

Rodney took a half-step back.

"They already know each other," Tucker said.

Wiley furrowed his brow. "How's that?"

Bobby nodded. "From back in the day."

"Was he your butt buddy in the joint like he was Tucker's?"

"Christ," Tucker said. "Why do you have to be such an asshole?"

Wiley shrugged. "Why is that wrong to ask? I always thought Rodney looked like a salad tosser."

Rodney winked. "Mary knows which way I swing."

"You sumbitch!" Wiley lunged at Rodney, but Tucker and Bobby latched onto him. The three pirouetted through the gravel driveway.

Rodney shimmied backward. "Maybe I'll toss Mary's salad tonight."

"I'm gonna kill you, you pervert!"

"Take it easy," Tucker said. "She's not worth it." He

patted Wiley's chest.

Bobby stepped away. "Looks like you boys have got some stuff to work out."

Wiley angrily motioned toward the garage. "Just get the stuff and take off. Leave your nose out of our business."

"About that," Bobby said.

"About what?" Wiley's face tightened as he breathed heavily.

Bobby jerked his head toward the garage. "I'm passing on this one."

Wiley's eyes narrowed. "What do you mean you're passing?"

Tucker moved closer to Wiley. Worry filled his eyes, and he glanced at Rodney.

"I mean," Bobby said, "I don't wanna do the job."

Wiley threw his hands in the air. "You drove all the way from Spokane."

"So I could tell you to your face."

"It's because of you." Wiley spun and pointed at Rodney. "What did you say to him?"

"Nothing," Rodney said.

Bobby waved his hands. "He didn't say anything. I'm just done. I decided it's no longer worth it."

"No," Wiley said. He smacked the bottom of his fist against the side of his head. "This doesn't make sense. You could have called to tell us."

The screen door opened, and Saxon stepped out. "What's all the yelling about?"

Wiley motioned toward Bobby. "He's pussing out. Doesn't wanna do the run."

Saxon shoved his hands into the pockets of his coveralls and walked over to Bobby. "Something happen?"

Wiley glared at Rodney. "It's 'cause of something baby

bird did."

"Hush yourself," Saxon said.

"I saw them talking."

The Old Man glared at Wiley until he looked down.

"Now," Saxon said to Bobby, "what changed your mind?"

Bobby shrugged. "You ever get a feeling somethin's about to go bad?"

Saxon studied him.

"Well," Bobby said, "that's what I've got. A premonition, if you will."

"Like someone walked over your grave?"

"Just like that."

Saxon pulled his lips back and bared his teeth. "Your father would deliver it."

"Transmission Jack can't deliver a newspaper these days."

"I heard the stroke made him about worthless."

"So did all those years in Walla Walla. He didn't listen to his gut when he should have." Bobby headed toward his truck. "I'm not going to make that mistake."

The four men stood there and watched the GMC turnaround and leave the Farm.

"What are we gonna do now?" Tucker asked.

"I'll drive whatever you need," Rodney said to Saxon.

"The fuck you will," Wiley said. "Don't let baby bird drive shit."

"Let me prove my worth," Rodney pleaded.

Wiley stepped forward. "Don't allow it, Saxon. I don't trust him. If you want, I'll drive."

"Ain't none of you drivers." Saxon headed toward the house. "Nolan will handle it."

***

The shadow of the Doghouse's peaked sign crossed the hood of Rodney McCready's truck. A caricature of a pit bull hung its head out of the opening and leered down on incoming customers.

Thumping music came from inside the bar, even though it was only a few minutes after five. The parking lot was fuller than normal, no doubt because of those folks attending the Stampede.

Rodney was about to speak into his cell phone when Bobby Tobeck noticed him sitting behind the steering wheel. He waved, then rapped his knuckles on the pickup's hood.

"All right," Rodney said. "So, that's it. Call me back when you get a chance."

He hung up and took the extra second to delete the call from his history. Rodney popped open the door and slid out of the driver's seat.

Bobby approached him. "Who were you talking to?"

"No one."

"I saw your lips moving."

"I left a message," Rodney said. Bobby's face registered confusion, so he added, "For a girl."

"The one you and Wiley were arguing over?"

Rodney hadn't seen Bobby in years, but he didn't want to lie to the man. The guy had tried to keep him out of trouble when they were kids. Had Rodney listened, he wouldn't have gotten arrested and gone to juvenile detention. Bobby later recommended Rodney avoid getting involved with a jewelry store heist. If Rodney had listened to Bobby then, he also would have avoided incarceration a second time. The men weren't close friends in those days, but both times Bobby looked out for him. That's why Rodney said something to him earlier at the Farm. Still, it didn't feel good to lie to him now.

"Wiley's got no shot with her," Rodney said. "She's made that crystal clear, but he's not taking it well." He thought about what Electric Mary had said after hiding the microphones in his apartment.

Bobby frowned. "Is she worth it?"

"I don't know. Maybe."

"Then why do it?"

"Because she's pretty." Rodney waved a hand. "And she likes having sex with me."

Bobby laughed. "That's enough reason in my book." He clapped Rodney's shoulder. "Let's get a beer and you can tell me why I'm running from Omak with my tail between my legs."

The two men left the sunshine for the Doghouse's neon-infused darkness. Beer and liquor signs hung on the walls, interspersed with canine-inspired paraphernalia. Movie posters for *Turner and Hooch*, *K9*, and *Old Yeller* commanded the most attention. Other pictures of dog breeds hung about the establishment. A large Gonzaga University poster proclaimed *This is Bulldog Country*.

Twangy music played over the raised voices of the patrons. An aroma of fried food and stale beer hung in the air.

"Been here before?" Rodney asked.

Bobby nodded. "Once or twice. Usually for a burger before I head back."

The two sat at a high table near the electronic dart boards and pool tables. No one was playing yet. The music was still loud in that area of the bar.

A server approached. She was in her mid-forties with

mousy brown hair and tired eyes. She had large breasts and a tight red T-shirt that read *My Boobs Thank You for Staring at Them*. "Get you something?"

"Pabst," Rodney said.

"Cheeseburger and a Coke." As if needing to explain his decision not to drink alcohol, Bobby added, "I've gotta drive back to Spokane."

"That it?" the server asked.

Both men nodded.

She walked away without writing anything down.

Bobby leaned forward. His expression hardened. "There better be a good reason why I walked away from that job."

Rodney looked down at his hands. He didn't know how to begin.

"It didn't feel good to lie to the Family," Bobby continued.

"Everybody lies."

Bobby leaned closer. "Did you lie to me back at the Farm?"

"No." Rodney shook his head. "I was trying to keep you out of trouble."

"What kind of trouble?"

"If I could tell you, I would."

Bobby pushed his baseball hat back on his head. "This is bigger than the stuff with Wiley."

"Much bigger."

"You got trouble with the law?"

"We all do. The best thing you could do is go home. Get as far away from here as possible."

Bobby rubbed his mouth. "If word gets out I quit on a job, it would cost me a lot of other business."

"That won't happen."

"How do you know?"

Rodney crossed his arms. "Because things are going to get bad here. When everything shakes out, no one is going to remember you walked away. If they do, they're gonna think you were some sort of shaman."

"That's a guy who sees the future, right?"

Rodney nodded.

"What if I tell Saxon what you told me?"

"It's not going to change anything. All it'll do is put you in the hot seat, too—for knowing me."

The server approached with a can of Pabst and a glass of soda. She set them onto the table. "Your burger will be ready in a couple minutes."

Bobby grabbed his drink. "No problem." When she walked away, his attention returned to Rodney. "The train has left the station is what you're saying."

"And it's gaining speed." Rodney sipped his beer. "The only way you avoid the collision is to get off the tracks."

Bobby stared at the dark liquid in his glass for a moment. "Now that I think about it, I'm not all that hungry. I think I'll grab something back in Spokane." He slipped off his chair. "It was good to see you, Rodney."

"You, too."

Bobby asked, "Why aren't you taking your own advice and getting out of town?"

"Because the train that's barreling toward us? I'm handcuffed to its caboose. I can't leave."

"Christ, man." Bobby stepped once and stopped. He looked unsure of what to say or do next. "Whatever you've gotten yourself into, I hope can find your way out."

"Me, too."

Bobby walked out of the bar without looking back.

In a moment, the server arrived with the cheeseburger.

She slipped it on the table. "What happened to your friend?"

"He had to go." Rodney pulled the burger to his side of the table. "I'll take the check when you have a minute."

10

A Strange Oasis

Mariam Coleman lived in the south end of town. The small yellow house had a clean yard and a white picket fence in need of a fresh coat of paint. It was a tidy home designed for minimal upkeep. The front door was open, and a screen kept out any pests.

The neighboring houses had similar construction and upkeep. No one was trying to outdo the proverbial Jones family, but they weren't trying to get left behind by them either.

Rodney pulled curbside, behind Mary's car. He honked the horn—three quick blasts.

His cell phone rang. Rodney tugged it from his pocket and saw it was Booster calling. He didn't want to talk with the club president at that moment for many reasons. The least of which was now at the front of the little yellow house.

The screen door swung open, and Electric Mary stepped out. She wore a half T-shirt, denim shorts, and black Converse with no socks. The woman oozed sexual confidence. For a moment, she paused in the doorway.

The cell phone continued to ring, and Rodney swiped his thumb over the screen to deny the call. He then waved Mary forward.

She glanced over her shoulder but didn't say anything to the people inside. She stepped away from the house and the screen door banged shut. Mary strolled down the pathway. She did her best to hide the confusion playing across her face.

Rodney reached over and unlocked the passenger door. Mary opened it and peered inside.

"What're you doing here?" she asked.

"Get in."

Mary's brow furrowed. "My mom's making dinner. You wanna stay?"

"We need to talk."

"What for?"

"Why do you think?"

Mary looked back at the house. Two older women peered through the front window. By their age differences, Rodney assumed they were Mary's mother and grandmother.

"Let's go," he said.

"Where?"

"Someplace private."

"We can talk here."

"You want your mom and grandmother hearing our business?"

Mary's shoulders slumped. "I should tell them I'm going."

"They'll see you leave."

She stared at him for a moment. "Whatever." Mary climbed into the truck and jerked the door closed behind her.

Rodney accelerated slowly from the curb.

Mary crossed her arms and leaned against the passenger door. Her gaze stayed focused out the windshield as Rodney piloted them through the small town. She remained silent for several moments, probably because she had assumed Rodney was taking her to his apartment.

When he diverted from that course, Mary asked, "Where we goin'?"

"I already said. Someplace private."

Her head swiveled about.

There weren't many private places to go in Omak. It was a small town in a mostly arid part of the state. However, there was a small forest on the southeast edge of town near the Okanogan River. Rodney went past it whenever he jogged.

Mary twisted in her seat. "Why aren't we going to your apartment?"

"I wanted someplace no one could hear us."

"You can just park the truck anywhere." She motioned toward the side of the road. "No one can hear us now."

Rodney drove down Ash Street until it dead ended.

"You're freaking me out," Mary said. "I don't know what you're doing."

He parked the truck. "Let's walk." Rodney climbed out and waited for her at the front of the vehicle.

Mary closed the passenger door. She wrapped her arms tightly around her. "Listen, Rodney. Why don't we talk here?"

Rodney waved at the neighboring houses. "Who knows if they're tied in with the Family?" He walked toward the edge of the trees.

She hurried up to him, her arms still clasped tightly around him. "The Family? What've they got to do with this?"

He held a finger to his lips. "Not yet."

It was a scraggly forest made up of sickly trees. The overhead canopy provided minimal coverage from the sun. However, the visibility from the street quickly decreased the deeper into the woods Rodney went. When he felt he'd reached the middle, Rodney stopped and looked around. He could no longer see the neighborhood they'd walked through.

Small, irritating bugs floated about his face. Rodney swatted them away.

The trees reduced the traffic noise from the nearby highway. Shadows crisscrossed the ground. It was a strange oasis in the middle of the city.

Rodney faced Mary. He gently held her by the upper arms. She looked up at him with her big brown eyes.

"I almost believed you," he said.

"About what?" Her brow furrowed.

"That you would do anything for me. That you'd be my perfect girl."

"I totally would." Mary's expression softened. "If you'd let me."

Rodney slapped her across her cheek. The crack echoed in the forest. Mary collapsed to the ground and her hands covered her face. Rodney grabbed her by the elbow and jerked Mary back to her feet. Dirt covered her arms and legs now.

Her left hand covered the side of her face as tears filled her eyes. "What'd I do?"

"Tell me you love me," Rodney said.

Mary's lower lip trembled.

"Go ahead. Tell me."

She swallowed and tears rolled down her cheeks.

"You don't love me?"

Mary shook her head.

Rodney smacked her on the opposite cheek. Mary squeaked and fell to the ground again. She curled into a fetal position and bawled.

"Do you know why we're here?" Rodney asked.

Mary hid her face in her hands.

"I know you hid the microphones in my apartment!"

She looked up at him through her spread fingers.

"That's right!" Rodney nodded. "I know!"

Mary scrambled to her feet and started to run, but Rodney kicked her in the ankle. Her legs twisted and she crumpled to the ground again. He jumped on Mary.

She struggled to get free, but the fight quickly left her. Rodney pinned her to the ground. When he grabbed her hair, Rodney expected Mary to scream, but she never did.

Rodney's face hovered over hers. "Tell me why."

Mary closed her eyes. "Saxon told me to."

"Did he pay you?"

She shook her head twice before nodding. "He gives my mother money."

Booster's words came back to him then. *The Family is bigger than you think.* Rodney released her hair. In a moment, he climbed off her. He brushed the dirt from his jeans.

"You owe him," Rodney said.

Mary sat upright. "A lot of us owe him."

"Like Dancing Arrow."

"Nancy hates the Family, but if Saxon wants something, she'll give it to him. Same reason as me."

"So he wanted you to bug my apartment. That's all?"

She shook her head.

"What else?"

Mary stood and brushed the dirt and forest debris from her body. "He wanted me to get close to you."

"All the stuff you said to me was a lie."

"Not all."

Rodney stared at her.

Mary lowered her gaze. "Maybe it started that way, but

I don't want it to be."

He sneered. "What does that even mean?"

"I don't even know what's true anymore." She pointed in the direction Rodney imagined The Farm might be. "There's a sickness out there and it's infecting us all. You, too."

"It's not infecting me," Rodney said defiantly. "I know who I am."

Mary rubbed her cheek. "You ever hit a woman before?"

"Never one I cared for."

Her eyes narrowed. "You cared for me?"

"I thought I did."

"Not now?" She reached for his hand, but Rodney pulled away. "I can still be your perfect girl."

"How are you going to do that? You're in the Family."

"So are you."

He shook his head. "It's different."

"Because I'm a woman?"

"I didn't make the rules."

Mary's eyes hardened. "No, you didn't. Maybe I'll quit."

"The Family?" Rodney cocked his head. "You can't do that."

"I can do whatever I want." Mary crossed her arms.

"What about the money for your mother?"

"There are other ways to earn."

"Like get a real job?"

She rolled her eyes. "Be serious."

"I've heard talk the Family's going to pull a job. You hear anything about that?"

Mary shrugged. "I overheard Kaylee and Tucker talking about something with the Renegades. You ever hear of them?"

Rodney nodded.

Mary shrugged. "That's all I know. They quit talking when they saw me. No one tells me what's going on."

Rodney looked up through the green canopy at the blue sky. He wondered what the Family was planning to do with the west side bikers.

Mary stepped closer and wrapped her arms around him. "I'm sorry for doing what I did." She laid her head on his chest. "I'll never do anything like that again."

He wrapped his arms around her. "It's okay," he lied.

"I promise to be your perfect girl." She nuzzled her head under his chin. "Forever."

***

Rodney reached for his apartment's doorknob to unlock it, but Mary grabbed him. Her arms circled around his neck and her body pushed him against the door. He closed his eyes and allowed himself to melt into her kiss. Rodney wrapped his arms around her waist. She moaned and pressed into him harder.

They kissed for a minute, maybe longer, until Mary reached for the keys in his hand. He let them slide from his fingers. Hunger filled her eyes as a lustful smile creased her lips.

Rodney turned his head slightly to watch the key slip into the lock.

"Listen," he said.

"Mmm?"

He covered Mary's hand and stopped her from unlocking the apartment.

Confusion replaced the desire in her eyes. "What's

wrong?"

"Hold on."

"Why?" The lust returned, and she kissed him again.

Rodney loved how her puffy lips felt against his.

Mary's hand struggled to turn, but he held it in place. She pulled back and opened her eyes. "What's wrong?"

"Once we go inside, they're going to hear everything we say. Everything we do."

Sadness filled Mary's eyes. "Let's throw them away."

"We can't. I need them to stay there."

She pulled her hand away from the lock. Rodney let her go.

"You don't have to come inside," he said.

"But I want to."

"I want you to, too." The words sounded funny in his ears and his face scrunched.

"Tutu," she said with a mournful smile.

"We can go somewhere else."

Mary lay her head against his chest. "It has to be here, doesn't it?"

"Not for you."

She looked up. "What's that mean?"

"They have to hear me inside. Moving about. Saying things to myself."

"Why?"

"So I can get into the Family."

Her lips twisted briefly. "It'll be better if they hear someone else in there with you. More believable." Mary stood on her tiptoes and lightly pecked him on the lips. "Let me help you."

She put her hand on the key still in the lock. Once more, Rodney covered her hand with his and stopped it from turning. Mary eyed him questioningly.

"I'm sorry," he said.

"It'll be all right."

"Not for that." Rodney jerked his head back toward the apartment. "For what happened in the forest. I shouldn't have hit you."

"Men have hit me before. Some I didn't deserve, but I'm pretty sure I deserved it from you."

"If I could take it back, I would."

Mary kissed him. "I know. Now, let me open the door."

Rodney's phone rang and he pulled it from his pocket. The caller ID screen showed a number he'd memorized. "Hold on," he said.

He thumbed across the screen and answered it. "This is Rodney."

"That's official," a male voice said. "Is someone listening?"

"That's right."

Mary cocked her head as she studied him.

"Can you call back later?" the man asked.

"Not right away," Rodney said. He smiled at Mary.

She tried to turn the key in the lock, but Rodney held her hand tighter now.

"You called," the voice on the opposite end of the phone said. "Is this something that needs a face-to-face?"

"That's right," Rodney said. "That would be great."

"How soon?"

"As soon as possible."

Mary's brow furrowed. She mouthed, "Who is that?"

"We could get up there tomorrow," the voice said. "Same place and time?"

"That'll work. See you then."

"All right," the man said. "See you then."

Rodney ended the call.

"Who was that?" Mary asked.

"A friend," Rodney lied.

"That's cryptic."

"Do you really want to know?" He let go of her hand.

Her tongue darted between her lips. "We can talk about it later. I still owe you your birthday present."

Mary twisted her hand, and the door opened. It banged against the inner wall as the two stumbled inside. She pressed him against the wall and clawed at his T-shirt. Rodney's fingers struggled to reach the door, but it was too far away.

He kicked his foot out, found the edge of the door, and shoved it closed.

11

Modern Day Cowboys

The cell phone's ringing woke Rodney. He lay on his back and stared up at the ceiling. He remembered he left the phone in his pants but made no move to answer it.

Mary pressed against his side. Her legs tangled with his and her arm draped across his chest. She lightly purred into his ear. Their uncovered bodies perspired in the morning's warmth. The day already promised to be a scorcher and sunlight seeped around the curtain's edges.

The ringing finally stopped. Cars traveled up and down Main Street. Rodney listened to their various engines, only picking out the occasional motorcycle as it roared by.

Voices drifted up from the sidewalk. In the short time Rodney had lived in Omak, he learned Saturdays were always busier. Out-of-towners visited to peruse the local thrift stores or boutiques. It was the ebb and flow of the little city.

However, the last few days were different. Many sightseers arrived to experience the Stampede. Rodney had heard about the event before moving there but never cared much about it. The whole Native American culture held little sway with him. He was sort of sympathetic to their plight, but he didn't care to learn about their history. He also didn't like westerns, country music, or mysticism. If he liked any of those, the Stampede might have held more allure.

The cell phone rang again, and Mary stirred. She

pressed her groin into his thigh. "Answer it."

Rodney didn't want to. He didn't want to have another cryptic conversation while being overheard by the Family's microphones. If he let the phone continue to ring after Mary told him to get it, that would seem weird, too.

He slid out of bed as the phone continued to ring. Rodney pulled it from the pocket of his jeans that were on the floor. The display screen showed it was Tucker calling.

Rodney answered. "Morning."

"No shit," Tucker said. "Something's wrong."

He eyed Mary as a host of worries rushed through his head. "What?"

"Nolan hasn't reported in."

Rodney left the bedroom. "What do you mean?"

"What do you think I mean? He should have reported in by now."

"If you say so."

"Why are you being an asshole?"

"I'm not," Rodney said. "I don't know how things are done. I'm not part of your inner circle."

Tucker sighed. "Yeah."

"Do I need to do anything?"

"No. Don't come out to the Farm today. Some of us are going to retrace his steps. Hopefully, he just had an accident or something."

Rodney stiffened.

"I know that sounds bad," Tucker said, "but what's the alternative? That the cops got him or worse?"

"What's worse than the cops?"

Tucker didn't answer.

Mary walked out of the bedroom. She was naked and rubbing the sleep from her eyes.

"Tuck," Rodney said, "what's worse than the cops?"

Tucker cleared his throat. "Saxon told me what Bobby said when he walked away from the job. You know, about someone walking over his grave? Maybe something bad happened to Nolan, like really bad."

Mary crossed her arms which pushed her breasts up higher. It wasn't a move to get Rodney's attention because concern masked her face.

Rodney looked down so he didn't have to maintain eye contact with her. He didn't want to explain to Mary what was occurring on the call at the same time as he was trying to learn what happened. "What's worse than the cops?" he repeated.

"I don't know, man. The feds, maybe."

Panic lanced through Rodney. "Are they watching the Farm?"

"No," Tucker said, "I don't think so. I'm just freaking out."

"Why? It's Nolan, right? He can take care of himself."

"You don't understand," Tucker said. "He's Mr. Reliable. He never does anything out of line."

Rodney looked up and stared at Mary. Her brow furrowed as she chewed on the side of her thumb.

"I'm sure everything's okay," Rodney said.

"Maybe." Tucker already sounded resolved that it wasn't.

"What do you want me to do?"

"I told you to stay out of trouble," Tucker said, "but I can see you're not taking that advice very well."

Rodney straightened. Was it just an expression or could Tucker see him? Rodney's gaze bounced around his apartment. Had someone in the Family hid cameras before sending in Mary to hide the microphones? Was Mary's getting caught part of a larger plan?

Or was Rodney twisting himself up? Was he inventing lies where there weren't any? The Family and the Wasted Souls masked their existence in lies. Rodney didn't need to make up any more to confuse the matter.

"I'm taking your advice," Rodney said.

"Christ." Tucker wearily scoffed. "It's a small town, man. Why are you messing with the one girl Wiley can't get over?"

Rodney remained silent now. Tucker had to know Saxon sent Mary to get close to him—didn't he? Or was Saxon testing the loyalty of everyone in his organization?

Mary moved closer now. Her hands settled on his waist as she searched his eyes for the truth. Concern and confusion mixed in hers.

"Be a little discreet, will you?" Tucker said. "Don't wave a red flag in front of the bull."

"I'm not sure how I can be any more discreet. We never leave my apartment."

Tucker sighed. "Hey, I gotta go. We'll talk about this later." He ended the call.

"That was Tucker?" Mary asked. "What did he want?"

Rodney set the cell phone on the coffee table. "Nolan is missing."

"Seriously?"

"Yeah. They're going to go look for him."

"Do you have to help?"

"No. He said for me to stay back today."

Mary tilted her head. "Because you're the new guy?"

"That, and they don't fully trust me yet."

"So, what did he tell you to do?"

Rodney pointed at the coffee table where he knew the hidden microphone lay. "He said for me to stay out of trouble." He grabbed Mary's hand and tugged her toward the couch.

"I think I can help with that," she said.

When he first kissed her, Mary melted in his arms and exaggeratedly moaned. She sounded like a new actress in a badly directed porn movie. Her cries of pleasure were too loud and too frequent. She continued like that for a while until the moans eventually became natural. That's when they both forgot someone from the Family might be listening.

***

Rodney and Mary showered, then went downstairs for breakfast at The Saddle Up Diner. The restaurant was full, and the din of conversation carried an excitement for the day's events. They waited near the front to be greeted. Rodney had never waited for service before.

Mary wore her clothes from the previous day. Rodney had changed into a clean T-shirt, but still had on the same jeans.

Carol approached after delivering a couple of plates to a table. "Gonna be at least thirty minutes." She motioned to a cluster of people mingling together on the sidewalk. "They've already checked in."

"We can go someplace else." Mary reached for the door.

Rodney shook his head. "This is the best place in town. We'll wait."

Carol winked. "I appreciate the loyalty. If you want, I'll have Woody fix you a couple of to-go plates right now. If you don't mind not eating here, that is."

"Let's do that," Rodney said.

They placed their orders and Carol walked off.

"What is it about this place you like?" Mary asked.

"They got free wi-fi."

Her brow furrowed. "That's it?"

"And the Monte Cristo sandwich is pretty good."

Her eyes flicked around the restaurant. "The cowboys and Indians stuff is too much."

Rodney chuckled. "The whole town is cowboys and Indians."

"That's my point." Mary turned to watch the customers outside. "Why do we hang around this town?"

"You tell me. I'm new."

She shrugged a single shoulder. "My family's here."

"You can move anytime you want. Just pick up and go."

Mary's gaze cut to him. "Where's your family?"

"No idea. They all left Moses Lake years ago. We lost touch after that."

She wrapped her arms around his waist, and Mary rested her head against his chest.

"Let's run away," she said. "You and me."

"Where to?" he whispered.

"Someplace where no one could ever find us."

He stayed silent.

Mary looked up at him. "Would you do that? Run away with me? We could be new people. Pretend we have new names."

Rodney kissed her lightly on the forehead. "I'd run away with you."

She smiled. "You could get a regular job. Become a real nine-to-five type. I'd be your perfect girl, just you see."

He knew it was a lie, not necessarily just for him, but for them both. Regardless, he liked the sound of it. They made small talk until Carol arrived with paper plates and plastic utensils.

Rodney paid for the meals and the two slipped out the door.

***

They ate as they walked along Main Street. Rodney balanced his plate in his left hand while he scooped eggs and hash browns with his right. Mary had tossed her plate into a trash bin since she ordered a breakfast burrito.

"I thought ahead," she said before biting off a chunk of the concoction.

Bumper-to-bumper traffic flowed north and south along Main Street while shoppers filled the sidewalks. Most dressed for the hot August day—shorts and light shirts. However, many wore casual western wear—plaid shirts, blue jeans, and boots.

Mary shook her head whenever they passed someone in a cowboy hat.

"What's your problem?" Rodney asked through a mouthful of eggs.

"You think they can even ride a horse?"

"I wear a baseball hat, but I can't hit a fastball."

She eyed him. "What kind of argument is that?"

He shoveled the last forkful of potatoes into his mouth. They followed a group of tourists and turned onto Omak Avenue. The traffic rolled slowly toward the Omak Stampede Rodeo Grounds.

"It's gonna be a hot one today," she said. "I didn't bring any sunscreen."

Rodney crumpled his paper plate. "Stay in the shade."

"There isn't any. You've seriously never been to the Stampede?"

"First time."

"A virgin." She slipped her hand into his. "Been a long time."

They crossed the bridge over the Omak River. The Stampede loomed ahead.

Loud, rumbling engines approached from the east. Rodney knew the distinctive sound and his pace quickened. It sounded like thunder due to the number of motorcycles.

"What's the hurry?" Mary said.

Rodney slowed when he caught sight of them. He didn't count the bikes. There were too many—it was larger than the Spokane chapter of the Wasted Souls, but Booster's crew mixed in with them. They left the arterial and headed for the parking field.

"Modern day cowboys," Mary muttered.

Rodney glanced at her as his pace slowed to almost a shuffle.

"Don't you think so?" she asked.

He hadn't expected Booster and the crew to be at the Stampede. This created a problem.

"You all right?" Mary asked.

"Yeah." Rodney forced a smile. "I'm doing great."

***

The Omak Stampede reminded Rodney of a county fair. A row of carnival games and smaller rides attracted the families. At night, it lit up like an arcade.

Even at this morning hour, an aroma of fried food and cooking meats drifted through the event. It mingled with the smells usually associated with horses and bulls—straw, dirt, and dung.

A teepee encampment sat on the eastern edge of the

fairgrounds. Native Americans dressed in culturally appropriate garb moved about the small tents.

Vendors hawking a variety of wares were everywhere. They sold T-shirts, local trinkets, cowboy art, Native American jewelry, and miscellaneous goods.

Rodney reached into his pocket and pulled out a twenty. "Here," he said to Mary. "Why don't you see if you can find some sunblock?"

She slipped the bill from his fingers. "Where you going?"

He thumbed over his shoulder. "Need to find a Honey Bucket."

Mary curled her lip. "Find me when you're done." She headed toward the vendors.

Rodney backpedaled until she was out of sight, then he spun and hurried toward the parking lot.

It wasn't hard to find the Wasted Souls. A cluster of Harley-Davidson motorcycles stood out in a sea of dusty pickups. Most had bedrolls attached to their bike seats. Men in leather vests lingered about.

As Rodney approached, he became more aware of the chance he was taking. If anyone local saw him, it would look suspicious. Two men in the club noticed Rodney. He didn't greet them, and they didn't acknowledge him.

Rodney walked by the club and continued to the row of blue portable toilets. He stood off to the side, so it looked as if he were waiting. In a moment, Booster sidled up next to him.

"You've been ignoring my calls," he said.

"There've been some developments." Rodney didn't look at the president of the Wasted Souls as he spoke.

Booster looked around as if searching for someone. "What developments?"

"That greenhouse I hit wasn't a Wasted Souls operation."

"No, it wasn't." Booster's voice held no remorse. "You did fine from what I heard."

It took everything Rodney had not to yell at the club president. His hands balled into fists, but he still looked straight ahead. "Why did you lie to me?"

"Because we needed to know how you'd do in a pinch."

Men entered and exited the porta-potties but neither Booster nor Rodney moved closer. They remained off to the side as if they might be waiting for a friend or a kid to finish their business.

"I could have been killed," Rodney said.

"But you weren't. You did good." Booster shifted his stance, and he continued to glance around. He never made eye contact with Rodney. "How much you take them for?"

"Twenty-four grand."

"That must've made Saxon happy."

Rodney clicked his tongue against the back of his teeth. "The opposite. The greenhouse belonged to the Savage Renegades."

Booster's chuckle sounded forced. "No shit."

"You knew."

"Watch the tone, prospect."

Rodney looked at Booster from the corner of his eye. "Saxon stole my money, then the son of a bitch tortured me."

Booster turned and studied Rodney now. "You tell him anything?"

"No."

The president's eyes narrowed. "How'd he know you had the money?"

"He's bugged my apartment."

"You found this out?"

Rodney nodded.

"Does he know you know about the bugs?"

"I don't think so."

"Smart. Continue to use it to your advantage."

Rodney looked away. "Why are you here?"

"You weren't calling. So, I figured I needed to come up and check on you. Some of the boys thought it'd be fun to tag along and catch the Suicide Race. We invited our Canadian brothers to cross the border and hang with us. You know? In the spirit of international relations."

"How'd you get rooms?" Rodney asked. "I thought everything was booked for the Stampede."

"We don't need rooms." Booster motioned toward the bikes. "We'll do fine with our bedrolls. That's if we can't find any locals to bed down with. None of the boys brought along their back-warmers so we're all gonna be on the prowl tonight."

Rodney hadn't noticed any women riding behind the Souls when they pulled into town. Maybe it was like Booster said—the chapter had come to town to see the Suicide Race and they weren't there to check on him. He was a lowly prospect after all. What did he matter in the scheme of things?

"Saxon do that to your face?" Booster asked.

Rodney nodded. "The Family doesn't trust me more than ever after the greenhouse job."

"Give it time," Booster said. "We don't trust you either, but you're coming along nicely."

"One of theirs went missing last night."

The president frowned and faced the portable toilets again. "Who's that?"

"Nolan." Rodney looked at his shoes. "You have

anything to do with that?"

Booster shook his head. "You haven't given me anything good enough to move on yet. When we come after the Family, you'll know."

"I just don't wanna be caught in the crossfire."

"Then answer your fucking phone." Booster glared at him now. "Otherwise, we might forget you're one of us."

The club president walked away.

12

An Associate, At Best

Rodney found Mary browsing through some jade jewelry at a small vendor shack. In her right hand, she held a spray can of sunscreen.

The proprietor, a fifty-something Native American, leered at her breasts as she bent over the encased offerings. His eyes darted to Rodney, and he straightened. "Good morning, chief." The man remained standing in front of Mary. "Help you find something?"

Rodney motioned to Mary. "I'm with her."

She glanced at him but remained hunched over the cabinets. "I was afraid you fell in."

The shopkeeper smiled. "She's got her eye on something." He stole another glance at her breasts.

"Looks like you got your eye on something, too," Rodney said.

The proprietor's grin vanished, and he backed away from the counter. He waved a hand at the jewelry case. "Let me know if you need help." He faded into the darkness of the booth.

Rodney bent next to Mary and examined the collection of jade jewelry. It all looked cheap to him, like junk someone could find along a roadside stop.

"What was he doing?" Mary whispered.

"Checking out your tits."

She craned her neck to peer down her T-shirt. "Huh." Her attention returned to the case. "What do you think about this one?" Mary tapped her finger above a tear-shaped necklace.

"You like it?" Rodney asked.

"I was thinking for you."

He smirked. "No."

She straightened. "Why not?"

"You see me wear any jewelry?"

"No."

"There you go." He pulled his phone from his pocket and checked the time.

"Miss a call?" she asked.

The shopkeeper lingered in the back of the booth but watched them with interest. Rodney slipped the phone into his pocket and wandered away.

Mary hurried to his side. "Have you heard anything about Nolan?"

"Not yet."

"If you want to help look for him, you don't need the Family's blessing. We can jump in your truck or my car and go looking for him."

"I wouldn't even know where to begin." Rodney looked at her. "Do you?"

"Not really, but I was trying to be helpful."

Rodney stopped walking and looked around the Stampede. "What do people do here?"

"You're looking at it." She waved her arm. "They wait until the rodeo starts. Tonight's going to be crazy because of the Suicide Race." Mary pointed at a cliff to the north. "That's where the horses will come over." Her hand swooped down like a plane making an emergency landing. "They come right through the river. It's a total sight, for sure."

"So people just mill about 'til all that happens?"

She nodded. "Pretty much." Mary lifted the can of sunscreen. "Let me spray this on you so you won't get burned."

He held out his arms and she misted the spray along them. Mary then squirted a blast of sunblock on the back of his neck and along his ears. "There," she said. "Now, you're safe."

"If only that were true."

"What's that mean?"

He slipped his hand into hers. "Let's go back to the apartment."

Mary didn't move. "Why?"

Rodney forced a smile. "Why do you think?"

"Maybe we can go somewhere else."

"Don't you want to be on the microphones anymore?"

She shook her head. "I didn't want to be on them in the first place." Her eyes softened. "I really don't want to be on them with someone I like."

"Why don't we cover the microphone in the bedroom? Maybe stick it in a shoe or something so they can't hear anything?"

"Maybe."

"It'll be better than hanging out in the sun all day."

Rodney led her away from the Stampede. He swiveled his head, looking for Wasted Souls and members of the Family. Not seeing any didn't make him feel better.

***

Rodney and Mary held hands as they walked. She tried to engage him in small talk—the type of stuff Rodney imagined citizens chatted about daily. It surprised him when Mary started down the path of hopes and dreams.

Her reputation made it sound like she never fell prey to hopeless romance.

She prattled on for a bit about finally getting her GED, then maybe trying for a two-year college degree from Wenatchee Valley College. When Rodney asked what she wanted to study, Mary shrugged.

"I don't know. Something that could get me behind a desk, I guess."

Rodney thought she could go to school for two years and learn enough so some company would allow her to answer their phones. He thought Mary was better than that and held her hand tighter.

They turned onto Main Street and walked among the people filling the sidewalk. A group of children up ahead were dressed like cowboys—even the girls. Each of them carried a stick with a wooden horse head on the end. They all pretended to ride them around their parents.

Mary smiled at them. "Someday I'd like to have kids."

Rodney eyed her.

"Maybe. I don't know. I think I'd be a good mom." She laughed at the face he made. "I definitely know all the things a kid shouldn't do." She bumped her shoulder into his. "You, too."

They walked in silence for a bit. Rodney never thought of himself as a family man. He certainly never thought of himself as a father. The idea of having a kid or a family with Mary was ludicrous. Rodney barely knew her. Besides, Saxon had used Mary to find out if Rodney was trustworthy.

He flexed his jaw and eyed her. Falling in love with the town whore was the dumbest move Rodney could make.

She caught him looking and smiled. Rodney immediately felt bad for what he'd just thought.

Mary squeezed his hand. "You ever want to be someone else?"

"Every day."

"Me, too," Mary said. "Except with you." She playfully bumped her shoulder into his.

They passed the used bookstore and Rodney glanced inside. "Hey, I'm gonna step inside and grab something new to read."

"I'll go with."

"Nah," Rodney said. "I'm gonna be a few minutes. It's how I am." He reached into his jeans and pulled out his keys. "You go back to the apartment, and I'll catch up."

Suspicion filled her eyes, but she took the keys.

Rodney pulled her in close. "I don't want you to be bored."

"All right."

He kissed her. They embraced with more passion than was customary on an Omak sidewalk. When they parted, her eyes filled with desire.

"Don't be long," she said.

"I'll make it quick."

Mary turned and strolled down the sidewalk. Rodney lingered for a moment and watched her go. She glanced back and caught him. It made her smile. Him, too.

He turned and pushed into the bookstore. A brass bell rang when he entered the store. Several customers drank coffee at the small round tables near the windows. They paid little attention to Rodney.

It was cooler inside courtesy of the store's air-conditioning.

Some soft '70s music played through hidden speakers. Even though Rodney disliked gentle rock, he enjoyed this song. It was about a guy on the run, hoping to get to the

Mexican border so he could be free again. He understood its message.

The smell of cooked coffee hung in the air. A small espresso machine stood behind the U-shaped counter. Rodney waved at the clerk as she cleaned the area. She was a kind woman in her mid-forties with short, graying hair. "Good to see you again."

"I need another book," Rodney said and pointed toward the back of the store.

"You came to the right place." The woman chuckled mirthlessly.

It was a needless exchange, but Rodney had them every time he visited the store.

He walked to the back of the store where the Mystery & Crime section was.

Another man stood there, studying a paperback. He wore a club shirt, golf shorts, and boat shoes. His dark hair was cut in a banker's style.

"You ever read this one?" FBI Special Agent Shane Walker asked. He held up Lawrence Block's *When the Sacred Ginmill Closes.*

"No." Rodney said. He glanced over his shoulder to make sure no one watched him talking with the lawman.

"Me neither."

Rodney faced the shelf and pulled a book out. He didn't even catch the title before he pretended to study the back copy. The two men stood side by side.

"What's going on?" Walker whispered.

"Did you grab Nolan?"

"The Canadian?" Now, Walker looked toward the front of the store. "No. Why?"

"Someone did."

The FBI man tapped the paperback against his hand.

"Maybe it was the locals."

"Nolan is careful," Rodney said. "He doesn't have a warrant. I'm not sure what reason any cop would have for detaining him."

"Was he running anything?"

Rodney nodded. "Another driver was supposed to move something for the Family, but he backed out at the last moment."

Walker raised an eyebrow. "Do you know why?"

"No idea," Rodney lied.

"What's this other driver's name?"

"Never heard of him."

"You didn't catch his name?"

Rodney shook his head.

"Huh." Walker tapped the paperback against his other hand again. "You think maybe this driver had something to do with Nolan's disappearance?"

Even though Rodney hadn't seen Bobby Tobek in nearly twenty years, he didn't believe the man would be involved in anything nefarious like that. Especially after Rodney had warned him away from potential danger. However, he said, "Who knows? Maybe."

"Is that all?" Walker asked. "We could have done this over the phone."

"There's something else." Rodney glanced toward the front of the store. "They're bugging my apartment."

"The Family?" Walker hunched. "How do you know?"

"One of them told me," Rodney said. "A woman." It was another lie.

"The Kaylee girl?"

"I haven't talked to you about this one."

"What's her name?"

Rodney waved a hand. "I want her kept out of the mix."

The agent's face pinched. "You're not directing the course of this ship." Walker tapped himself in the chest with the paperback. "I'm the captain. You work for me." Now, he tapped Rodney in the shoulder with the book. "Got it?"

Rodney didn't like the FBI man. He especially didn't like it when Walker reminded him of their power dynamic. "Yeah. I got it."

"You're the one trying to stay out of prison. Remember?"

"How can I forget?"

Walker smirked before turning back to the bookshelf. "What's her name?"

"Electric Mary."

The FBI man scrunched his nose. "What kind of name is that?"

"That's what they call her."

"What's her real name?" Walker wriggled his fingers.

"I don't know," Rodney lied. He lost track of how many he'd told since walking into the bookstore. That was how he lived his life now—a lie within a lie within a bigger lie.

"What does this Electric Mary do for the Family?"

Rodney paused before answering. "She's like me."

Walker scowled. "The Family's got her watching you?"

"That's right."

"She the one who bugged your apartment?"

Rodney nodded. "She also told me about them, so I figure it's a wash."

"How are they monitoring them?" Walker must have noticed the confusion on Rodney's face because the agent continued. "The microphones won't have great range, so someone's got to be sitting nearby listening to what's going on. Keep an eye out for any suspicious looking vehicles around your apartment.”

Rodney winced at the embarrassment he felt. He should have realized that before the agent told him. “Will do.”

“Them bugging you says they still don’t trust you. Any reason why that’s not improving?”

“Maybe because I’m a rat.”

“They don’t know that,” Walker said.

The bell tinkled and both men craned their heads toward the front of the store. Two older women entered the bookstore and headed for the counter. Maybe they wanted to order coffee.

“Okay,” Walker said. “Be careful what you say inside your apartment.”

“Thanks for the tip.”

Walker wrinkled his nose. “Don’t be sarcastic. It’s an important precaution.”

“Maybe we should end this whole thing now.”

“Call off the operation?” Walker rolled down his lower lip. “We can do that. It’s no skin off my nose. I’ll do up the paperwork and you can return to prison. How’s that?”

Rodney shoved the paperback he was holding onto the shelf. “Never mind.” He selected a new book to pretend to study.

“I thought so,” Walker said. “What’s going on with the Souls?”

“They’re up here today.”

“What for?”

“I didn’t call Booster back.”

Walker’s eyes hardened. “Why not?”

Rodney couldn’t tell him about the greenhouse incident and his desire to avoid Booster because of it. “I was busy.”

“Don’t lose sight of your mission, Rodney. We want the Souls.” Walker waved the paperback. “Getting something on Saxon and the Family is a bonus. The Souls are the prize. If we can't deliver a bust on them, the operation is a failure and our deal with you is kaput."

"I'm trying."

Walker leaned in. "Try harder. I don't have the budget to keep you up here forever."

Rodney stepped away. "Find out about Nolan. I need to know if the cops have him."

"All right." The FBI man lightly tapped the book against Rodney's arm. "If you need anything today, a couple of my friends and I will be around. We thought we'd check out the rodeo and the Suicide Race before heading back to Spokane. None of us has seen it before."

Great, Rodney thought. Not only were the Wasted Souls going to be in town all day, but so was the Federal Bureau of Investigations. It was a greatest hits collection of his worst problems.

"You're not getting a room?" Rodney asked.

"Everything's booked. Not even the U.S. Government could finagle a hotel room. So, it'll be a late-night drive home."

Rodney nodded once, then headed toward the counter to pay for his paperback. He didn't even recall the title he had picked out. It wasn't the first time that had happened.

"Anything else?" the clerk asked.

"I already got more than I bargained for," Rodney said.

The clerk studied the paperback. "*High Country*?" She spun the book so Rodney could see it. "Didn't you already buy this one?"

He forced a smile. "I did. This one is for a friend."

"Nevada Barr is great, isn't she?"

"You bet," he lied. He hadn't read the first copy he purchased.

The clerk tapped the register and announced a total.

****

Rodney walked up Main Street. Usually, the sidewalks weren't clogged with pedestrians. Even the last two days, the run-up to today's Suicide Race, hadn't caused that much increase in activity. Right now the restaurants and businesses seemed full of visitors.

He passed The Saddle Up Diner. Several families milled about on the sidewalk, waiting for their turn to get breakfast.

The bumper-to-bumper traffic heading toward the Stampede moved at a snail's pace. The cars heading away sped as if fleeing a crime scene.

Rodney searched for any suspicious vehicles parked around his building like Agent Walker had suggested. Was a cargo van with thousands of dollars of listening equipment necessary? Technology was so small and affordable nowadays any member of the Family could sit in any car and listen to the microphones planted in his apartment.

Could Saxon have tied the microphones into The Saddle Up's wi-fi like Rodney did? Maybe. If he did that, then the Family could listen to the bugs back on the Farm. Rodney doubted the microphones were tied into the internet. Not because Rodney knew anything about the bugs, but because the Family was low-tech. Even though they had the latest cell phones, everything else about the group seemed simple.

As Rodney turned the corner onto Bartlett Street, he continued to search for suspicious vehicles and for trucks belonging to the Family. Half a block away, an old U-Haul truck was parked curbside. A sun shield blocked its front window. He'd never noticed it before, but he hadn't looked for any suspicious vehicles either.

Rodney continued past his apartment building to get a better look at the truck. If someone was sitting inside the back, they'd likely be miserable. No shade protected the truck and the sun glinted off the metal roof. It would be hot as hell in there.

A low rumble sounded in the area, but Rodney couldn't immediately place it. He got within fifteen feet of the truck and realized the noise was from a small generator. It was likely attached underneath the truck or to its roof. Whoever was inside the back was probably running a small air-conditioner.

Rodney turned and headed toward his apartment.

Could whoever was inside the truck see him? Or were they only able to listen to what was going on inside his apartment?

Did they need to be in the truck the whole time or could they just check it periodically? It seemed like a waste of manpower to have any of the Family members sit inside the cargo truck and listen to his activities. Maybe they followed him until he returned home. That bothered him. Were they tailing him wherever he went? Did they do that with anyone new to the Family? Or was it just him? If it was the latter, why?

Rodney started up the stairs to his apartment and paused.

Wasn't the Family supposed to be looking for Nolan? That's what Tucker had said earlier in the morning. If that were the case, who was in the old U-Haul rig?

Rodney stole a glance back at the moving truck.

Who was even telling the truth anymore?

Rodney lied to the Family, and they lied to him. He understood why. He wasn't in their inner circle, and they needed to protect their secrets. If they allowed him into the Family, maybe they'd finally be honest with him.

Booster lied to Rodney about the greenhouse, and Rodney murdered two men because of it. Rodney had lied to the Wasted Souls first about his intentions for joining the club. He tried to join their world so he could avoid another prison sentence.

He stopped outside his apartment.

Mary, Rodney thought. She'd lied to him, too. Now she was honest. At least, Rodney believed she was being truthful. He had no way to know for sure, except in how she kissed him. Was that a hokey reason to believe? It probably was.

Which left Special Agent Walker as his only source of truth. Rodney's shoulders slumped. Cops lied more than anyone—it was the only universal fact.

Rodney entered the apartment and locked the door behind him.

"Mary?" he called.

"In here."

She was in the living room, sitting on the couch.

"What happened to your clothes?" Rodney asked.

"I was hot."

"Yes, you are," he said with a lascivious smile.

***

A crash against the front door caused Mary to straighten abruptly from her position on the couch. The back of her head violently collided with Rodney's face, forcing him off her. It felt she had just walloped him with a large hammer.

He stumbled into the coffee table, catching the top of his calves. He lost his balance, turning his world upside down. Rodney rolled backward over the table and collapsed onto the floor.

"You okay?" Mary asked. She ran around the table to help him.

Something slammed against the front door again.

Rodney pushed himself to his hands and knees. Bile rose in his throat.

Mary looked toward the front of the apartment. "Who the hell—"

The door splintered open after the third crash. Heavy footfalls stomped through the apartment. Wiley Jones rounded the corner. He stood before the naked Rodney and Mary.

Wiley wore a black Whitesnake T-shirt, blue jeans, and untied combat boots. His curled cowboy hat was pushed back on his head. Wiley carried a nasty-looking revolver in his right hand.

"Goddamn you, Rodney!"

"Wiley," Rodney croaked. It was all the defense he could muster. His world had yet to stop spinning after the reverse headbutt from Mary.

"Get out!" she shouted.

Wiley kicked Rodney in the arm, and he collapsed helplessly to the ground.

"You knew I loved her!" Wiley hollered. "I even told you so!"

"Leave him alone!" Mary cried.

Wiley pulled off his straw hat and swatted her with it. "Stay outta this, bitch! Or I'll shoot your ass, too."

Mary jumped away from Wiley's angry slaps.

"Don't shoot," Rodney said. He pushed himself off the floor.

"Don't tell me what to do." He bent and pushed the revolver against Rodney's head. "I'll shoot you if I want to."

Rodney eyed the man around the barrel of the gun. "You need Saxon's approval."

Wiley shoved the gun harder into Rodney's head. "Maybe he told me to do it."

"He didn't."

Outside a car honked and someone yelled in response.

Wiley looked at Mary. She self-consciously wrapped her arms around herself.

"Please," she said, "don't."

"Whatever." Wiley lowered the gun.

Rodney leaned back on his haunches and put his hands on his thighs. He forced a smile as the world titled at a severe angle. "Family hurting Family."

Wiley pointed the gun at Rodney's exposed groin. "You don't know what you're talking about."

Bile again rose in Rodney's throat. He awkwardly covered himself as he swayed. It was a futile gesture since a bullet would still rip through his hands and blow off his manhood.

"Why are you here?" Rodney asked. His eyes fluttered and his voice sounded as if it were coming from the bottom of a well. Everyone's did.

"Yeah?" Mary chimed in. "Why are you here?"

"Saxon said to get you," Wiley said.

"Why didn't you call?" Rodney stood. He felt wobbly.

"I thought it would be more fun to surprise you." Wiley's eyes hardened and he waggled his gun. "And look at what I found. Two dirty lovebirds." His eyes darted to

Mary. "You never got into it with me like that."

"Leave her alone," Rodney muttered.

Wiley lifted the gun higher at Rodney, but his concentration remained on Mary. "You think she loves you, Rodney? She don't. She's gonna break your heart. Believe me. She's a stone-cold bitch."

Mary glanced at Rodney. "That's not true."

"Anyone find Nolan?" Rodney asked.

"Get dressed." Wiley lowered the gun. "Then get your ass out to the Farm."

"What about me?" Mary asked.

Wiley smirked. "You've done enough damage for today." He left the apartment then.

Rodney stumbled after him. When he got to the door, he closed it, but it wouldn't latch. The door jamb had splintered near the lock. He'd need the landlord to fix it, or his apartment would remain unsecured while he was gone all day.

"What are you going to do?" Mary asked.

"Go to the Farm."

"Are you okay to do that?"

"Not really." Rodney lowered himself to one knee. His head hurt.

Mary reached out and touched his shoulder. "What happened?"

"You," he said as he laid on the floor. "You happened."

"What'd I do?"

13

Born Yesterday

Rodney pulled off the highway and drove slowly toward Saxon's house. Dread filled him as his truck crept forward.

The nausea had stopped before he left his apartment. Rodney worried he might have a concussion. Light bruising formed on the left side of his cheek up to his forehead. Mary had smashed his face good when she jerked her head back. It was an accident and there was nothing he could get mad at. On another day, he might even laugh at it.

However, he needed to deal with the Family and doing so while feeling like he just got into the ring with a young Mike Tyson wasn't ideal.

He parked his truck near the others. Rodney paused long enough to notice Tucker's pickup was missing along with Nolan's. Only Wiley's and Kaylee's remained. Saxon's was usually inside the garage.

Rodney slipped out of the driver's seat and headed toward the house. He was about to pull the door open when he realized he'd brought his cell phone with him. Rodney grimaced. It was the concussion or whatever was one degree less than that.

A mid-coitus headbutt? Whatever it was, Rodney was off his game.

He turned back to his truck. He didn't want to bring the phone into the house. Not only did Saxon forbid him to have one on the property, but he was expecting a message from Agent Walker about Nolan's status.

The screen door to the house opened. Wiley stood there with one hand on the lever. The other held a bottle of Pabst. "Where you going, baby bird?"

"Back to my truck."

"What for?" Wiley kicked the bottle back as he swigged a healthy drink of beer.

"I forgot to put my phone away." Rodney motioned toward the truck. "House rules."

"Bring it." Wiley pushed the door wider. "C'mon. Saxon's waiting."

Rodney's stomach tightened, and he thumbed at his pickup. "It'll only take a minute."

Wiley's expression darkened. "What'd I say?"

"All right." Rodney stepped by Wiley as he moved into the house. "Where's Tucker?"

"If he was in your ass, you'd know."

"Huh?"

Wiley passed him on the way through the kitchen. "Get yerself a beer."

"I'll pass."

"It's your funeral."

Rodney followed Wiley into the living room. Sunlight seeped around closed curtains and light flickered from the television. A cigarette haze hung above everything.

Saxon sat in the recliner opposite the TV. A glowing cigarette dangled between two fingers and an ashtray balanced on the armrest.

Kaylee sat cross-legged on the couch facing the living room. She wore another T-shirt and a different pair of denim shorts. Both looked too big for her thin frame. She barely acknowledged Rodney when he entered the room.

Instead, she lifted a cigarette to her lips and inhaled. Its tip glowed red.

"Have a seat," Saxon said. He motioned to the position on the couch nearest him.

Rodney sat where directed.

Wiley dropped onto the couch with Kaylee, across from Rodney. Neither Wiley nor Kaylee made a sniping comment at the other. Instead, they watched Rodney like children prepared to hear a sibling's punishment.

The Old Man inhaled on his cigarette as his attention remained locked on the television. "You've been busy," he said. Smoke slipped from his lips as he spoke.

Rodney stayed silent and studied the Old Man, hoping to find any indication for being beckoned to the Farm.

"He brought his phone," Wiley tattled.

Saxon's eyes cut to Rodney, and his lip curled. "You know the rules."

"I was going to put it in my truck."

The Old Man's face tightened. "Why didn't you?"

"Wiley said to bring it."

"I never said that." Wiley innocently touched his chest. "Why would I say something that?"

"Put it on the table."

Rodney pulled it from his pocket and laid it face down on the coffee table.

Saxon stared at the phone. He inhaled once on the cigarette, then exhaled. He sniffed before leaning toward Kaylee. "Turn it over. Make sure it's not recording."

She untangled her legs and snatched the phone from the table. Kaylee stuck her cigarette in her mouth so she could work the device with both hands. "What's your password?"

"Zero eight one one," Rodney said.

Kaylee's fingers tapped in the code. She looked up but cocked her head to avoid the cigarette smoke drifting into her eyes. "That's yesterday's date."

"My birthday," Rodney said.

"Born yesterday." Wiley chuckled. "Fucking classic."

Saxon wriggled his fingers at Kaylee. "Well?"

She squinted. "He's not recording nothing."

"What about his call records? Who's he been calling?"

Kaylee's fingers danced over the phone's screen. She inhaled on the cigarette and blew the smoke from the corner of her mouth. "He ain't called nobody but us."

"We know that isn't true," Saxon said. "Don't we?"

Wiley laughed. "Deleting your call history like a cheating husband."

"Besides you all, the only person I called is Electric Mary." Rodney faced Wiley. "But you know that."

Wiley jumped to his feet. "I should have kicked your ass harder—"

"Her number is in here," Kaylee said.

"Sit down, Wiley." Saxon crushed his cigarette in the ashtray. "Nobody is kicking nothing until I say so. Got it?"

"Yeah," Wiley said dejectedly. He dropped onto the couch. "I got it."

The Old Man wriggled his fingers again at Kaylee. "No calls to or from no one we know?"

She shook her head. "Nope."

Saxon turned to Rodney. "So this friend who told you about the greenhouse. What was his name again?"

"Henry Wade," Rodney said.

"Why's his name not in your phone book?"

"Because I thought there might come a moment like this."

The Old Man leaned to the side and fumbled in the

recliner's pocket. When he straightened, he removed a snub-nosed revolver. Saxon rested his elbow on the chair and pointed the gun at Rodney's face. "What's the boy's number?"

Rodney stared at the Old Man. His hand tensed around the armrest. He'd sunk into the couch cushions. There was nowhere he could go in a hurry. Any move would be a struggle. Rodney was a sitting duck.

"Tell us the number so Kaylee can call it," Saxon said. "If the guy on the end of the phone doesn't identify himself as Henry Wade, I'm gonna blow your head off."

Wiley chuckled. "Happy belated birthday."

"He's not going to answer," Rodney said.

Saxon straightened his arm, which brought the gun closer to Rodney's nose. The barrel looked huge now, like looking down the tube of a cannon.

"After the greenhouse incident," Rodney said, "Henry told me never to contact him again. He said he was changing his number and leaving town." It was an easy lie, but not a very good one. At least, it rolled off Rodney's tongue without much trouble.

The Old Man's eyes narrowed, and he lowered the gun. "The greenhouse incident. That's cute. You're downplaying your involvement in a couple murders."

"I'm not downplaying anything."

Kaylee looked up from Rodney's phone. "What's Intruder Defender Plus?"

Rodney eyed her. "A game."

"No, it's not." She tilted the phone so Saxon could see. "It looks like some sort of video program, but it's not accessing anything." Her attention returned to Rodney. "Why not?"

"Lemme see," Wiley said.

She rotated the phone so the other man could view it.

Saxon lifted the gun again. "Well? What's the problem?"

"My data service doesn't roam," Rodney said.

"What's that mean?" the Old Man asked.

"Means he needs to be connected to some wi-fi," Kaylee said. Her fingers bounced over the keyboard. "I'll take care of that."

Everyone sat in silence for a few moments. Rodney's attention drifted to the television. *Judge Judy* played on the screen. When Kaylee said, "Got it," he turned away from the staged court proceedings.

Her mouth opened, and she looked up at Rodney. "You bugged your own apartment. Why?"

"I'm paranoid."

Saxon leaned forward. The gun almost touched Rodney's head. "She asked you why."

"You don't trust me," he said. "I don't trust you."

Kaylee turned the phone to the Old Man again. "He must have seen us."

"Stealing my money?" Rodney asked. He nodded. "Yeah. I saw."

"You came here pretending you didn't know." Saxon lowered his gun. "So you lied."

"Everybody lies. I'm just protecting my ass."

An engine roared up the driveway. Wiley cocked his head. "Tucker's back."

The Old Man smiled. "Protecting your ass. That might be the most truthful thing you've said since we met." He dropped the gun into the side pocket of the recliner. Saxon grabbed the pack of cigarettes and shook one free. "Now, we're going to get to the bottom of this."

Tucker entered the house and headed for the bathroom.

Wiley glanced at Saxon, then at Rodney. He grinned with barely contained malice.

Rodney grabbed the armrest and tensed his legs. He leaned forward and inched himself toward the edge of the couch. He wanted to be prepared to move quickly. Rodney didn't want to get caught mushed into the cushions again.

Kaylee shifted, bringing her legs up underneath her. She closely watched Rodney and didn't look up as Tucker entered the room. Rodney couldn't wiggle any further toward the edge of the couch without her seeing. He froze in an awkward position.

A cell phone buzzed. Rodney tensed, worried it was his. However, his cell phone was face up on the coffee table and the screen remained dark. When the buzzing occurred a second time, Rodney realized it came from the Old Man.

Saxon shifted in his chair and pulled out his phone. He answered it with a simple, "Yeah?" His face tightened. "You sure? Uh-huh. How many of them? Interesting. No, no. Thank you for the call." After he hung up, he said, "The Wasted Souls are in town."

"The fuck for?" Wiley asked.

The Old Man shrugged. "The Stampede, it seems."

Concern filled Kaylee's eyes. "That a problem?"

"I don't think so."

A toilet flushed and a door opened. Footsteps paused in the kitchen before passing through the living room.

Saxon lifted his chin, and his gaze followed Tucker into the room. "How was the drive?"

"Uneventful," Tucker said.

The late arrival came into Rodney's line of sight now.

As he did, Tucker handed three CDs to the Old Man. He walked around the coffee table and dropped between Kaylee and Wiley.

"That's how they sent it?" Wiley asked. "They didn't have a VHS tape available?"

"Shut it," Tucker said. He twisted the cap off his beer and tossed it on the coffee table. He eyed Rodney as he kicked the bottle back for a long swallow. "What's up your butt?"

"He's getting ready to make a run for it," Kaylee said.

Saxon's empty hand dropped off the side of the recliner. "Sit back."

Wiley's hand had slipped behind his back. "Nah. Let him run."

Rodney released his grip and he flopped onto the couch. His chin touched his chest. He was in a worse position than before. Now, his face hurt again from where Mary hit him.

Saxon's hand reappeared from the recliner pocket, and he turned his attention to Tucker. "You see the videos?" He spread the CDs apart like a man fanning a handful of cards.

Tucker swallowed another mouthful of beer. "Yup."

"And?"

"He put 'em down." Tucker pointed his bottle at Rodney. "Like we thought."

Rodney pushed himself upright on the couch. If he was going to die today, he didn't want to do it slouching.

"He give them boys any chance?" Saxon asked.

Tucker shook his head. "None. To be fair, one drew on him first."

"He should never have been there in the first place." The Old Man fanned the CDs as if cooling himself. "You know what we got here?" He directed the question at

Rodney.

Rodney nodded. "Video from the greenhouse."

"That's what it is," Saxon said, "but what's it represent?"

He mumbled his answer.

The Old Man's brow furrowed. "Say it louder. My ears ain't as young as they used to be."

"My freedom."

Saxon wiggled the CDs. "They represent more than that."

"My life."

"Bingo. Your life."

Rodney shifted on the couch, still trying to get himself back into an upright position. "I pulled the job for you." His gaze swept over those sitting on the couch. "For you all. To be part of the Family."

Saxon laughed. "Don't con a con man, son. You've been lying from the jump." He leaned to his left and set the discs on the table next to Kaylee. "Why don't you start from the beginning?"

"I'm not following."

"Okay," the Old Man said. "How about this one. Who sent you here?"

Rodney shook his head. "No one." He motioned toward the others. "I was in town and ran into Tucker at Kaylee's party."

"Right," Saxon said. "You were in town. Why was that again?"

"I was looking for work."

"In Omak?" The Old Man leaned on the armrest. He stared at Rodney like a prosecuting attorney. "You came to work the farms, is that it?" He glanced at Tucker. "You didn't tell us ol' Rodney here was a wetback."

Tucker's lip curled. "He's no beaner."

"That's what I figured." The Old Man's gaze settled back on Rodney. "No white man comes up here to work the fields. You sure as hell ain't no Native. Try again."

"Fine. Spokane was hot. I already told you."

Saxon snapped his fingers. "That's right. You mentioned something about that. Some bullshit about being in trouble with the law. What'd you do again?"

"I robbed a bank."

"A bank." Saxon chuckled. "One that didn't go so well. You didn't get away with anything. Did you?"

Rodney had gotten away with some money, but he hadn't got far. The distinction didn't matter now.

The Old Man rolled his hand. "You needed to get away from Spokane which is why you ended up here."

Something in the way Saxon said it caused a chill to run down Rodney's spine. Did he know Rodney's secrets? Or was he just fishing?

Rodney's cell phone buzzed a single time on the coffee table and the screen briefly lit up. It was the signal a text message had arrived.

Kaylee reached for it.

"What is it?" Saxon asked.

She entered Rodney's password, and her thumbs bounced a couple of times on the screen. "You're not going to believe this," she said absently.

Tucker leaned closer to read the phone.

"What am I not going to believe?" Saxon asked.

Rodney grabbed the armrest. Even though he was sunk into the couch, he'd have to attempt a run for the door.

"Don't even think about it," Wiley said. He leveled his gun at Rodney's chest. "I'll get you before you stand."

Everyone turned to study Rodney.

Once more, he let go of the armrest and settled back into the couch.

"It says—" Kaylee shifted the phone so Tucker could read along with her.

He bolted to his feet. "You fucking rat."

Saxon held up hand. "Let her read it."

Tucker pointed at Rodney. "He's a fucking rat."

Wiley jumped to his feet. "Lemme shoot him."

The Old Man waved his hand. "Nobody's shooting nobody until I hear what's on that phone."

Kaylee stared at Rodney. "How could you?"

Rodney lifted his hands in surrender. "I can explain."

Tucker motioned toward the phone. "You can't explain that!"

Wiley set one foot on the coffee table and leaned forward. "Just one bullet is all it'll take."

Saxon clapped his hands once. The sudden jolt caused everyone to focus on the Old Man. His face pinched. "Read the fucking text," he said to Kaylee.

She nodded several times. "Nolan Tremblay arrested for DUI collision outside Wilbur. WSP responsible."

Wiley clucked. "We know this." The gun drooped in his hand. "What's the big whoop?"

"There's more," Tucker said. "Read it."

Kaylee inhaled deeply as if steeling herself for something terrible. She swallowed. "It says, 'Call to discuss Nolan's viability as a potential witness.'"

Wiley brought his other foot onto the coffee table. Beer bottles fell over, liquid spilled out, and dribbled onto the carpet. Wiley loomed over Rodney and pointed the gun down at him. "You fucking rat!"

"Don't shoot him!" Saxon ordered.

"Why not?" Wiley barked.

"Because we need answers." Saxon eyed Kaylee. "Who's it from?"

She turned the phone so the Old Man could see. "It doesn't say. There's no name. Just a number."

Saxon twisted in the recliner. He leaned over the armrest and glared at Rodney. "Who's it from?" Spittle flew from his lips. "And don't lie to me, boy. Now's not the time."

Rodney pushed himself upright in the squishy couch. He didn't want to die slouching. "It's from Special Agent Shane Walker."

"The FBI?" the Old Man asked.

Rodney nodded.

"Oh, Christ," Tucker said. He shoved his fingers into his hair.

"Lemme blow his head off!" Wiley shouted. He whipped the air with his gun.

The Old Man lifted a hand as he struggled to get out of the recliner. "What's the FBI want with us?"

"Nothing," Rodney said. "Not really."

Saxon's lip curled. "Don't tell me *nothing*, boy. I wasn't born yesterday."

"No, you weren't," Wiley said. He squatted on the coffee table. The devil was in his eyes. "That was Rodney."

14

Bad Blood

Rodney grabbed the armrest and attempted to pull himself off the couch. He didn't get far.

"No," Saxon said. "You stay there."

Wiley hopped off the coffee table. "Nuh-huh, princess." He pushed the table back away from him with an angry shove of his legs.

"Hey!" Kaylee and Tucker hollered in unison. They lifted their feet to avoid the table smacking them in the shins.

Tucker clambered over the table to stand next to Wiley. Kaylee crawled over the edge of the couch to join Saxon.

Rodney's world had tumbled in on itself. The four of them surrounded him and he was in an inferior position with no weapon. In fact, his gun was at the bottom of the Columbia River. In order to save himself, he'd just outed himself as an FBI source. It was going to be a genius decision, or it was going to be further proof that everything he touched turned to trash.

He patted the air with both hands. "I can explain."

"You'll do that in spades," Saxon said. "I promise."

Tucker kicked the couch and jostled Rodney. "We were friends!"

"I told you." Wiley grinned. "Didn't I tell you? There was something off with this guy."

Saxon hooked his thumbs on the bib of his overalls. "Does this Agent Walker know about—" The Old Man cocked his head. "What did you call it—the greenhouse affair?"

"The greenhouse incident," Kaylee suggested.

Saxon nodded. "Does your federal agent know you murdered two men?"

Rodney stared at the Old Man, doing his best not to give anything away.

"That's what I thought." Saxon pointed at the CDs on the end table. "What if we delivered those to the FBI? That'd fuck up your whole world—wouldn't it?"

Rodney swallowed.

"You remember what happened in the barn?" the Old Man asked.

"Yes," Rodney said. His voice sounded small. He didn't bother trying to make it sound tough.

"That's when we didn't know anything. That's when we still liked you. Think about what we'd do now. We wouldn't stop until we get the story—the *whole* story. Understand?"

Rodney nodded.

Tucker kicked the couch again. "We shared a cell!"

Wiley laughed. "You vouched for him."

Tucker spun and stuck a finger in Wiley's face. "He fucked your girl."

Wiley jammed his gun in Tucker's belly. "Say it again!" Spittle flew from his lips. "I dare you!"

"Not now!" Kaylee shouted.

Rodney grabbed the couch and moved to stand. It was a stupid decision. Not only was it four against one, but Wiley still had his gun out. Before Rodney could get to his feet, Saxon kicked him in the shin. Rodney howled and fell back onto the couch. He grabbed his injured leg.

Wiley brought the gun around and pointed it at Rodney.

"What're you going on about, baby bird?"

The pain in Rodney's leg was excruciating. His fingers interlaced over the shin, and he held it the way a child does after skinning a knee. He continued to groan loudly.

"Shut up and listen," the Old Man said.

"Hey!" Wiley hollered. "Stop your squawking. Saxon asked you a question." Wiley whipped the gun barrel across the top of Rodney's forehead.

The world exploded inside of Rodney's skull. He squealed and grabbed his face. He brought his legs up into a fetal position on the couch. The side of his face already hurt from Mary's reverse headbutt, but now it felt like a nail had been hammered into his head.

"Did I tell you to do that?" Saxon bellowed over Rodney's wailing.

"He wasn't talking," Wiley yelled.

"Shut up," Tucker hollered. He kicked the couch again. "Goddamn baby."

Wetness leaked between Rodney's fingers, and he knew it was blood without looking. His eyes remained shut and his squealing dropped to a low moan. The nausea returned, and bile rose in his throat.

"I think he's going to barf," Kaylee said.

"Sit up," Saxon ordered.

Rodney's lips trembled, and his stomach tightened. He wasn't going to be sick. It was worse than that. He knew the troubling signs. It had happened before.

"I'll get a bucket," Kaylee said, "and a towel for the blood."

"Is he crying?" Wiley asked with a chuckle. "Oh my God. Look. He is."

"Get up," the Old Man ordered.

Tucker kicked the couch once more. "Fucking pansy."

Rodney remained on his side with his eyes closed. The slick wetness between his fingers grew. The blood now mixed with his tears. If they killed him, he no longer cared. He just wanted it to be quick. He wanted the hurt to stop.

"You two," Saxon said. "Get him up."

"Not me," Wiley said. "I got the gun."

Two hands grabbed onto Rodney. "I'm never gonna forgive you," Tucker said. He jerked Rodney upright.

"Look at me," the Old Man ordered.

Rodney kept his hands over his face and his eyes remained shut. He was a crying ostrich with its head in the sand, a bawling gopher hiding in its hole. If he couldn't see the Old Man, then the threat wasn't real.

Blood and tears ran down the bridge of Rodney's nose and along his left eye socket.

"Don't make me hit you again," Wiley said.

Rodney lowered his hands and looked at Saxon. The vision in his left eye was blurry from blood. He sniffled and tried to control his sobbing.

"Christ," Wiley muttered.

"You got him good," Tucker said. "Serves him right."

Saxon put his hands on his knees and leaned forward to study Rodney. He didn't bother looking at the cut on Rodney's forehead, but rather the Old Man searched his eyes. It was as if he was looking deep into Rodney's soul.

Rodney was afraid Saxon would find only one thing—weakness.

The Old Man sneered. "I'm going to give it to you straight, boy."

Nasty saliva formed in Rodney's mouth, and he struggled to swallow it. He blinked repeatedly.

"This is going to end badly for you," Saxon continued. "Maybe not here and now, but it will. Mark my words."

"Fuckin' A," Tucker said. "Nobody rats out the Family."

Wiley leaned to get a better view of Rodney's forehead. "Is that bone?" he muttered.

Kaylee returned to the room with a bucket and a towel. She dropped both into Rodney's lap. When she saw his forehead, she pulled back. "Holy shit."

"I know," Wiley said with a grin. "Right?"

Rodney clutched the bucket to his chest with his left hand. With his right, he pressed the crumpled towel to his forehead.

Saxon straightened. "How you choose to go out is up to you, Rodney. You want to go out like a mouse, or you want to go out like a man?"

***

Saxon crossed his arms. "Let's start over. What's this business of the FBI not wanting us?"

Rodney spat into the bucket. "I didn't say they didn't want you."

"Oh, here we go." Wiley waved the gun. "The bullshit begins."

The Old Man held up a hand. "Let him talk. He knows how this goes if he lies."

The barn, Rodney thought. He didn't want to go back out there.

Rodney stared at the Old Man. "You're gravy."

Saxon cocked his head. "Gravy?"

Tucker kicked the couch. "What the hell does that mean?"

"Mind not doing that?" Rodney asked. It was amplifying his headache.

"This?" Tucker's eyes widened and he booted the couch. "You don't like this, huh?"

Rodney winced.

"Easy," Saxon said.

Tucker kicked the couch again. "How about that? Want some more?"

Wiley laughed. "Make him barf."

Rodney looked into the bucket. "I'm sorry." His voice echoed in the plastic pail.

"Tucker," the Old Man said. "That's enough."

"He doesn't tell me what to do." Tucker pointed at Rodney.

"He's not," Saxon said. "I am. We're trying to get to the bottom of this. Okay?"

Tucker spread his arms. "That's all I'm saying."

The Old Man turned back to Rodney. "Why are we gravy?"

"Because the feds want the Wasted Souls."

Wiley jabbed his gun in the air. "Whatever, Keyser Söze. Try again."

Rodney got the reference to the movie *The Usual Suspects*, but it appeared Saxon missed it. He stared at Wiley.

"He's bullshitting us," Wiley said. "He said their name because he heard they were in town."

"The Souls are in town?" Tucker asked.

Wiley rolled his eyes. "Keep up."

A commercial for an Erectile Dysfunction pill started on the television. Saxon snapped his fingers then wriggled them. "Somebody turn that horseshit off."

Kaylee spun and hunted for the remote. She found it next to the CDs. In a moment, the TV shut off.

Saxon's upper lip curled as he focused on Rodney. "The

Souls?"

Wiley clucked. "You're not believing this."

The Old Man waved at him frantically. "Hush yourself." He eyed Rodney once more. "Well?"

Rodney nodded once. "That's right."

Saxon turned slightly to study the CDs on the end table. When he faced Rodney again, he asked, "How are you affiliated with them?"

"I'm a prospect."

Tucker looked toward the ceiling. "You gotta be kidding." His gaze dropped to Rodney. "When did this happen?"

"After we got out of Coyote Ridge."

Saxon cocked his head. "You weren't riding with them before?"

"No." Rodney spat a glob of nasty saliva into the bucket again. "I got into some trouble after we got out. That's when the FBI showed up."

The Old Man tapped the armrest. "Because of the bank job gone bad?"

Bile rose in Rodney's throat, and he vomited into the bucket. Tears filled his eyes and his headache pounded worse than before. He pressed the towel harder to his forehead.

Wiley laughed. "Payback is the best."

"Shut up," Saxon barked. He waved at Rodney. "Answer my question."

Rodney cleared his throat and spat into the bucket. "The ATF and the FBI want the Souls for running guns across the border."

Saxon stiffened. "What have they got on them?"

"I don't know."

Tucker kicked the couch. "Not good enough."

Rodney flinched. "I don't know how much they've got. Walker didn't tell me."

Saxon scratched his cheek as he thought. "How'd they get you connected to the Souls. I'm not seeing it."

"My cousin," Rodney said. "He's patched in."

"He vouched for you?" Tucker asked. "So, you made him an asshole just like you made me?"

Kaylee shifted her stance. "What's the relationship to us?" She looked at Saxon. "We've never worked with the Souls."

"Bad blood," the Old Man said.

"How's that?" She glanced at Tucker and Wiley and they shrugged in return.

"It's between me and Booster," Saxon said, "their current president. He was just a thug back then. Goes back a couple decades."

The Old Man sat on the recliner. He grabbed his pack of cigarettes and shook one free. After he lit the cigarette, he blew the smoke toward the ceiling.

"Care to fill us in?" Wiley said.

Saxon waved his hand. "The Souls wanted to run their guns in and out of Canada, but I never trusted the bastards. I especially didn't trust Booster who was trying to score points, climb the ranks so to speak." He inhaled on his cigarette again. "Booster and I butted heads, had a couple of skirmishes. This was back in the nineties. Nothing you all would know anything about. I thought it was gone and forgotten."

Kaylee grabbed the pack of cigarettes and pulled one out. "What're we going to do about this?"

"I'm thinking," Saxon said. "Gimme a minute."

Rodney leaned back against the couch. The nausea was passing but the pain in his head was excruciating.

Wiley sat on the edge of the coffee table. He rested his elbow on one knee and let the gun dangle between his legs.

Tucker crossed his arms and stared at Rodney, muttering to himself.

Kaylee lit her cigarette. "Let's go to Canada." Smoke escaped her lips as she spoke.

"They extradite," Wiley said.

She waved the smoke away from her face. "We haven't been charged with anything."

"Those Canucks can't be trusted," Wiley said. "They'd send us home in a heartbeat if the FBI wanted us. No, we gotta go elsewhere."

"Or stand our ground," Tucker said.

Kaylee and Wiley looked at him.

"Butch and Sundance style." He held his hands out, miming guns with his thumbs and forefingers.

"None of us are dying today," Saxon said.

Wiley lifted his chin toward Rodney. "What about him?"

"That remains to be seen." The Old Man inhaled on his cigarette. "Here's what we're gonna do. Tucker, I want you to call Electric Mary. Have her come out here."

Rodney stiffened.

Wiley stood and faced Saxon. "Why you having him call her?"

The Old Man's face tightened. "Why do you think?"

"I don't know," Wiley said, his words sharp. "Why don't you tell me?"

Kaylee interrupted. "Because she won't come if you call her, creeper." She tapped the side of her head. "Think for once."

Wiley pointed at her. "Watch yourself."

"You watch yourself." She inhaled on the cigarette.

"Go on," Saxon said to Tucker. "Call her and get her over here."

Tucker pulled his cell phone from his pocket and walked out of the room.

"Why you bringing her out here?" Rodney asked.

Saxon raised an eyebrow. "Your time for asking questions is over."

Wiley sat on the coffee table once more. "Rats don't get to ask questions."

"Kaylee girl," the Old Man said, "take those CDs and wipe them down with some glass cleaner. Make sure there are no fingerprints anywhere on them. Got it?"

She stuck her cigarette between her teeth. "On it."

The Old Man waggled a finger at the discs. "Put 'em in a paper bag when you're done."

Kaylee grabbed the CDs and left the room.

"While we wait," Saxon said, "tell me what the FBI knows about our operation."

Rodney stared at the ceiling. "They don't know much."

"That's not what I asked. Tell me what they know—*exactly*. We need to know how much damage control is needed."

"They know this is a waypoint," Rodney said. "What more could I tell them? I don't know any more."

"Booster didn't tell you anything?"

Rodney shook his head. "He just said, go up and infiltrate the Family."

"That's the word he used—infiltrate?"

Rodney nodded. "He said if I did that, I'd get patched in."

Saxon crushed his cigarette out in the ashtray. "That's why the FBI let you come up here. It's the long game for them. You infiltrate us—" The Old Man air-quoted infiltrate. "—and you're made a Soul."

"That's the way I figured it."

Saxon lowered his head for a moment. The chuckle started as a low rumble. It soon grew into a full-throated roar. "That sumbitch." The Old Man slapped his hands together.

"What?" Wiley asked.

"He knows." Saxon pointed at Rodney. "Somehow Booster knows you were a rat. He sent you up here to take the heat off the Souls."

Rodney's shoulders tightened. It couldn't be. There's no way Booster could have known he was working with the FBI.

The Old Man smiled as the realization set in for Rodney. He wriggled his fingers in front of Rodney's eyes. "I see it settling in there. That's why Booster told you to hit the greenhouse. Think it through." Saxon nodded slowly as his eyes filled with glee. "If you get killed doing robbing the greenhouse, what's the harm? If you're successful, you hurt a Savage Renegades operation. Plus, the whole caper is hanging over your head. Win-win-win."

"No," Rodney muttered.

"If you were really successful, the FBI would come and haul us out of here." Saxon's eyes grew distant. "Ol' Booster. The dirty son of a bitch. He almost got away with it."

"You're believing him?" Wiley asked.

"That Rodney is a Wasted Soul?" Saxon nodded. "No truer words have ever been spoken."

15

Proper Motivation

Rodney no longer thought about running. What was the point?

Saxon and the Family could destroy his life if he got away or if he stayed. They had video footage of him robbing the greenhouse. Worse, they had evidence of him murdering two men. Kaylee was still in the kitchen making sure the CDs didn't contain anyone's fingerprints. If Saxon indeed intended to turn over the discs to the FBI, he'd want to make sure none of the Family had left any tell-tale evidence behind.

Even if Rodney managed to destroy the CDs, he couldn't be sure that was the end of it. The Savage Renegades likely kept a copy of the video somewhere. Maybe at the greenhouse. Perhaps even on the cloud. Rodney would never be free of the digital evidence.

Soon Mary would be there.

Tucker hadn't returned to the room yet, but Rodney was sure Mary would answer his call. Everyone liked Tucker. Once the Family got her out to the Farm, Saxon would use her as leverage. Rodney wanted to believe he didn't care about her, but he knew the truth.

Saxon crushed his cigarette in the ash tray and immediately reached for another one. He stuck it between his lips, and it bounced as he spoke. "You get paid for being a rat?"

Rodney clutched the bucket tighter to his chest, and he

pressed the towel harder to his forehead. He wanted to collapse in on himself and vanish from this existence.

Wiley was back on the other couch with his feet on the coffee table. The gun lay sideways on his knee, its barrel pointing directly at Rodney's face. One flinch of Wiley's finger, and Rodney's bad day would be over.

"Well?" Saxon snapped the lighter and inhaled through the flame. Smoke escaped through his lips.

"No," Rodney said. "They're not paying me."

"So, you're ratting for free?"

"I'm staying out of jail."

"You've done time before." Saxon studied the burning end of his cigarette. "You could do it again."

Rodney stared into the bucket. The acrid smell of his vomit wafted up. It was better than meeting the Old Man's judging eyes.

Kaylee returned to the room. She wore white cotton gloves and carried the CDs in her left hand and a small, brown paper bag in her right. She stopped next to Saxon's recliner.

"All clean?" the Old Man asked.

"Like they've never been touched."

Saxon inhaled on his cigarette, then motioned with it toward Rodney. "Have him finger them."

Kaylee flicked her wrist and the paper bag opened, filling with air. She fanned the CDs with her left hand and extended them to Rodney. "Pick a card."

He took a CD and held it in the air.

"Press your thumb on it good," Wiley said.

Saxon waggled his hand in Rodney's direction. "Both sides. Don't make it hard for the cops to find where you touched it."

There was no use arguing. Rodney turned the disc in his

hand and mashed his fingers against both sides. Kaylee extended the bag, and he dropped the CD into it.

She held out the other two CDs. "Next."

Rodney picked one and pressed his fingers against it.

"The other hand, too," Saxon said. "Get some blood on those discs."

Wiley chuckled. "Lots of blood."

Even though his left hand had touched his head after Rodney hit him, most of the blood had dried or been wiped off on the side of the bucket. None appeared to have been transferred to the first disc. When Rodney removed the towel from his forehead, the skin briefly stuck to it.

Kaylee grimaced. "That's gonna need stitches."

Rodney dropped the towel on the couch next to him. He gingerly touched his forehead and felt torn skin. Blood covered his fingers. He rubbed them together before manipulating the CD.

Kaylee held out the paper bag and Rodney dropped the second disc into it.

They repeated the process for the final disc. After he dropped it into the bag, he grabbed the towel and reapplied it to his head.

"What do you want me to do with these?" Kaylee asked Saxon.

"Put them there." The Old Man pointed at the end table nearest him. "Then get him a bandage. Bring a bigger paper bag this time, too."

Kaylee dropped the little sack on the end table and left the room.

"Not even going to fight, baby bird?" Wiley asked.

Rodney grunted. "What's the use?"

He bounced the barrel against his knee. "Checkmate, motherfucker."

"It's only check," Saxon said as he crushed out his cigarette. "He's still got outs." The Old Man's eyes cut to Rodney. "Ain't that right?"

Rodney didn't see a way to escape his predicament except to go along with whatever Saxon had planned. Maybe that's what the Old Man meant.

Tucker returned to the room.

"Where the hell you been?" Wiley asked.

"Calming down." Tucker dropped onto the couch near Wiley. His jaw flexed as he glared at Rodney.

"Doesn't look like it worked," Saxon said.

"You didn't bunk with the man."

"Aw," Wiley said with a mocking laugh. "Still a couple butt buddies."

Tucker smacked Wiley across the chest and the gun fired.

Rodney screamed as a burning sensation ripped through his left shoulder. He dropped the towel and covered the injury with his right hand.

Saxon bolted from his recliner. "You moron!"

"It's not my fault," Wiley shouted. "He hit me."

Rodney howled in pain. His shoulder felt on fire.

Tucker said, "What's the big deal? He deserved it."

"I got plans for him," the Old Man yelled. He leaned over Rodney. "Where'd he hit you?"

Kaylee sprinted into the room. "What happened?"

Saxon pushed Rodney's head to the side and pulled his hand away from the injury. "The fool shot Rodney."

"It's not my fault," Wiley repeated.

Rodney wanted to shout for the Old Man to get off him but right now he hoped for some help.

Saxon jerked Rodney forward. "It just clipped the meat. No bone. You're lucky."

"See?" Wiley said. "Not so bad."

The Old Man glared at Wiley. "I was talking about you, dummy. You're the one who's lucky."

"But Tucker hit me," he said weakly.

Saxon now eyed Kaylee. "We're gonna need more bandages. Bring the needle and thread, too."

She dropped the large paper bag and single bandage she'd brought onto the table.

"What do you want us to do?" Tucker asked.

The Old Man glowered at him. "How about you both pull your heads out of your asses?"

Wiley and Tucker exchanged glances.

"Go outside," Saxon said, "and wait for Mary. Keep her out there until we're done fixing what you caused."

Tears filled Rodney's eyes as he stared at the ceiling. Wiley and Tucker bickered on the way out of the living room.

Saxon hovered over him. One hand pressed against Rodney's chest while the other cupped the injured shoulder. "I'm gonna give you a way out of your trouble, prospect."

Rodney's gaze slid to the Old Man. He looked like a rattlesnake waiting to strike.

"At first, you're not gonna believe I'm helping you," Saxon said, "but I am. Trust me. I know what I'm doing. I've been in these situations before."

Tears rolled down Rodney's cheeks. What the Old Man said sounded like a lie, but right then Rodney didn't care. He wanted it to be the truth because hope glimmered in Saxon's words.

***

Rodney lay on his stomach on the coffee table. The surface felt cool on his skin. His bloody T-shirt was crumbled on the floor. It wasn't a comfortable position, but he'd already been on the table for some time. Kaylee kneeled next to him as she worked.

While he was on his back, she sewed the entry wound closed. Kaylee also put several stitches into his forehead. She'd brought a bottle of whiskey along with her supplies. Rodney took several gulps initially, but it didn't help with the pain. It did calm him, though. Right now, he bit on a stick as she continued to close the hole in his shoulder.

Saxon quietly sat in the recliner and watched them.

A car arrived at the Farm, but no one entered the house. Occasionally, muffled voices floated into the room, but Rodney couldn't make them out.

Kaylee had a steady hand, but she didn't have any bedside manner. She didn't ask how Rodney felt, if anything she did hurt him, or if he'd like another drink of whiskey. Instead, Kaylee jammed the needle into his skin and angrily tugged on the thread, provoking a groan from Rodney as his jaw tightened further around the stick.

It seemed as if she delighted in causing those small explosions of pain. Some stabs of the needle were harder than others; some jerks of the line were more intense than previous ones. Kaylee never lightened her touch until she cut the string and applied a bandage. It happened like that on the front of the shoulder and the forehead. Kaylee smoothed the last bandage.

She slapped the wounded shoulder. "Done."

Rodney winced and he bit on the stick. It cracked between his teeth. He moaned in agony.

"What would we do without you?" Saxon asked Kaylee.

She stood. "Probably bleed to death."

Rodney opened his mouth, and the stick fell to the ground. A line of thick saliva clung to it.

Saxon leaned forward. "Put the towel and bloody bandages in the big paper bag. The stick, too. His saliva is all over it."

"Right." Kaylee collected the items the Old Man listed without hesitation or revulsion. She shoved them all in the large brown bag.

Rodney sat upright on the coffee table. The movement made him light-headed. Carefully, he reached for his T-shirt.

"Leave it off," Saxon said. "Just a little longer."

Kaylee dropped the sack next to the Old Man's recliner.

"Tell the boys to bring in Mary," Saxon said.

She nodded. Before Kaylee could leave, Saxon grabbed Kaylee's arm and pulled her down to whisper into her ear. When the Old Man finished, Kaylee left the room without looking back.

"Feeling better?" Saxon asked Rodney.

"That's not how I'd describe it."

"You're lucky to be alive. Rats have notoriously short lifespans."

Rodney nodded once. "So I hear."

The door to the house opened. A moment later, footsteps wandered through the house. Tucker entered first, followed by Mary and Wiley. Kaylee didn't return with them.

When Mary saw Rodney, she took a quickened step toward him but caught herself. She stuttered to a stop. She must have realized something was wrong. Her eyes darted about the living room, checking the faces of the Family members. When Mary's gaze returned to Rodney, her brow furrowed.

"Your boyfriend's in a heap of trouble," Saxon said.

Wiley stepped forward and extended an arm in front of Mary. "Rodney ain't her boyfriend."

The Old Man's lip curled, and he stood. "Get yourself under control, Wiley. This night almost went bad because of you."

"Me?" Wiley pointed. "Tucker had a hand in it."

Tucker shrugged. "Get mad at me all you want. Rodney's the rat. Let's not forget that."

Horror splashed across Mary's face and her gaze flitted about the room. "What?"

"A cheese eater," Tucker said. He kicked a table leg and jostled Rodney. "Aren't you?"

"No." Mary covered her mouth with her hands.

"Just getting it, huh?" Wiley motioned repeatedly at Rodney. "Baby bird's an FBI informant."

Mary's eyes widened further.

"Understand?" Tucker asked. "You bedded a rat."

"Hey!" Wiley shouted.

She muttered, "How I was I supposed to know?"

Tucker's lip curled as he eyed Wiley. "You heard her moaning. You know she loved it."

Wiley grabbed Tucker by the shirt and balled his other fist. "Take it back!"

"You two," Saxon shouted, "knock that shit off!"

Tucker and Wiley froze in their mutual hate.

Mary spun to Saxon and pleaded, "I would never."

"I know," The Old Man said. "It's all right."

"You asked me to—"

"Enough!" Saxon barked. "Hold your tongue, girl."

Mary straightened, a little girl scolded. Her eyes darted to Rodney. "How could you?"

Nausea rolled over him. Rodney wondered how much of it was from guilt and how much of it was from the adrenaline leaving his system now that Kaylee had finished stitching him up. He wanted to throw up.

"I said things to you!" Mary cried.

Wiley let go of Tucker's T-shirt. "What'd you say?"

Rodney lowered his head.

"What'd you say?" Wiley repeated.

"Get up," Saxon ordered.

Tucker kicked the coffee table. "You heard him."

Rodney stood on unstable legs.

The Old Man motioned to Mary. "Scratch him."

She froze. "What?"

"We know how mad you are," Saxon said. "Hit him, scratch him. Let the rat have it."

"They're setting us up," Rodney said.

The Old Man punched him, and Rodney dropped back to the coffee table. He'd been hit harder in the face before, but the strike still surprised him. It hurt worse than it should have because of the earlier headbutt and the pistol whipping.

Tucker booted the table leg and jostled Rodney. "On your feet, rat."

Rodney pushed himself upright.

"I'm giving you a way out," Saxon said. "This is just your motivation." Rodney started to argue but the Old Man held up a single finger. "I told you to trust me, but you had to go off spouting. Do it again and there's no deal."

Rodney nodded. His tongue darted across his lips, and he tasted blood.

Mary remained rooted to the ground. Fear filled her eyes.

Saxon waved her forward. "C'mon, girl. Time to step

up."

"Wait a minute," Wiley said. "Is what he said true?"

The Old Man sneered. "Get with the program, Wiley, or take your ass outside."

"I need to know—"

"Outside!"

Tucker shoved Wiley away. "You're screwing up, man."

Wiley pointed at the Old Man. "What you're doing ain't right."

Saxon stepped away from the recliner. "I swear to God—"

"Just go," Tucker said.

Wiley raised a defiant hand. "I'm going." His eyes cut to Tucker. "Why don't you say something? You know this ain't right." Wiley muttered to himself as he left the house.

When the door closed, Saxon's eyes refocused on Mary. "It's okay. Just a couple of scratches."

Tears filled her eyes. She looked scared. "Why?"

"Because I said." Saxon's eyes hardened. "What more do you need?"

Tucker's face pinched with anger. He stepped forward and shoved Mary. "Do it already."

She shuffled like a zombie with her eyes locked on Rodney's.

He didn't say anything as Mary approached. The world swooned and he felt like falling. The Old Man grabbed his arm and held him steady.

"Dig those nails in," Saxon said.

Mary dragged her fingers over Rodney's chest. Confusion replaced the fear in her eyes.

"Deeper," the Old Man said.

"Draw blood," Tucker encouraged.

"I can't," Mary said.

"You can." Saxon shook Rodney. "Remember, he's an informant."

"A dirty fucking rat," Tucker offered.

Rodney met Mary's questioning eyes. He nodded, then looked toward the ceiling.

She wailed as her fingernails dug into his chest. They dragged down across his abdomen.

"That's it," Saxon said. "Again."

The pain returned to Rodney's chest as Mary's crying intensified. Her fingernails sliced down to his torso.

"Now, hit him," the Old Man said.

Mary sniffled. "I don't want to." She stepped back.

"He won't hit you back."

Rodney closed his eyes and set his jaw.

"No," Mary said through sobs. "Please."

"You don't want to hit him? That's all right," Saxon softly said. "Pull some of his hair out."

Rodney lowered his gaze to her.

Mary blinked away tears. "I can't."

"This is bullshit," Tucker said. He stepped forward, grabbed a clump of Rodney's hair, and yanked. He held the bloody mass like a prize.

"Throw it in the bag with the towel," Saxon ordered.

Tucker stepped around the coffee table and wriggled his fingers. The hair fluttered into the bag.

Kaylee returned to the living room. Once again, she wore white cotton gloves. This time, however, she carried a revolver.

Rodney clearly saw the play now. Once his fingerprints were on the gun, they could kill Mary with it. His DNA was underneath her fingernails. They had a clump of his hair, his blood on a towel, and his fingerprints on the CDs.

Any detective in the world could make a case with that evidence. Once the cops saw the videos on the discs, the case against Rodney was a certified slam dunk. The prosecuting attorney could write his closing statement before lunch.

Kaylee extended the gun to Rodney. He didn't argue against holding it. As soon as it was in his hand, Rodney pointed the revolver at Saxon.

The Old Man frowned. "If you want your way out of this trouble, you've got to trust me."

Rodney pulled the trigger, and the gun clicked. He pulled the trigger several times. *Click, click, click.* There were no rounds in the cylinders.

Kaylee snatched the revolver from him. "Stupid ass," she grumbled.

"I don't understand what's going on here," Mary said.

Saxon patted Rodney's good shoulder. "We've just given Rodney the proper motivation to hold up his end of the bargain." The Old Man faced Rodney. "Ain't that right, prospect?"

Now, there was something that confused him. "What bargain are we talking about?"

"That's what we're about to discuss."

16

Better the Devil You Know

Getting to the rodeo was a pain in the ass. Even though traffic was bumper to bumper, most everyone seemed in a good mood. That angered Rodney. His body hurt and he didn't want to be in this mess. He had called Booster and asked for a place to meet.

"The Stampede," he said. "We're still here. Call when you arrive."

Which he did. Rodney was to meet the club president in a park-like area to the east of the grandstands. Finding it was easier said than done. The carnival and its rides operated to the south. The Indian encampment was spread out across the baseball and soccer fields.

Ogling families shuffled along while laughing. Partying cowboys strode about. Happy young couples walked slowly among stone-faced Natives.

Calliope music from the carnival rides floated playfully through the air until it smashed into the '80s glam rock pumped out by various food trucks. The aroma of cooking meat combined with the smell of untold spices to create a mystery bouquet—a foreign concoction no chef could recreate in a single kitchen.

Rodney stumbled through the crowd. He ignored the suspicious or concerned looks. There hadn't been time to clean up the blood and to change his shirt. Right now, he was on a mission.

His goal was simple—to save his life and his freedom.

Mary factored into that equation, too. If he wasn't alive and free, he couldn't save her. At least, that's what he kept telling himself.

Rodney didn't want to admit it, but he'd put everything at risk for the woman. He knew she was affiliated with the Family. She wasn't an angel and had played him from the beginning, but he believed she might have feelings for him. He thought he might have them for her, too.

At the east end of the grandstands was a cluster of trees. Rodney headed in that direction. When he neared, the crowd thinned, and he finally saw the park. Rodney slowed and, for a moment, thought about running in the opposite direction.

Booster wasn't there alone. The entire Spokane chapter of the Wasted Souls was with him, too. So were the Canadian brothers.

Axel spotted Rodney first. He tapped Booster on the upper arm and the club president turned.

"Let's go," Booster hollered. He waved his arm for Rodney to hurry up.

Overhead, the stadium's PA system kicked in. "*Ladies and gentlemen, boys and girls, welcome to the Stampede!*" Applause followed the announcement. The announcer continued in a Native language Rodney couldn't understand. Extra applause followed, albeit smaller and more polite.

Rodney walked over toward the park.

"*You're in for real treat tonight,*" the announcer said, "*the world-famous Suicide Race!*"

The crowd's cheering grew substantially louder.

Booster's face pinched. "We gave up our seats for you."

The rest of the Souls glared at Rodney, even Axel. It was as if they all wanted to tear Rodney's head off for making them miss the start of the rodeo. Rodney had no idea the Souls were fans of cowboy stuff.

"They didn't have to," Rodney said.

"You asked to meet. Said it was important. I figured it had to be about Saxon." Booster's eyes narrowed and he moved closer to Rodney. "What happened to your face?" He noticed the blood on Rodney and the hole in his shirt. "Were you shot?"

"That's what I needed to talk to you about."

Booster studied the top of Rodney's head, probably where Tucker had yanked some hair out. He turned to Axel. "Make us some privacy."

Axel whistled, then spun his hand. "Cone of silence."

The bikers formed a circle around Booster, Axel, and Rodney. Each man stood shoulder to shoulder, but they all looked away. None talked amongst themselves. As rodeo attendees passed by, the bikers discouraged any looky-loos with comments like, "Nothing to see," "Move along," and "Mind your fucking business, pal."

Booster crossed his arms. "All right, kid. Lay it out."

"Saxon knows I'm working for you."

The club president's expression darkened. "How'd that happen?"

The lie tumbled from Rodney's lips by habit. "I don't know."

Booster frowned. "You don't know?"

"No."

The club president looked at Axel. His head movement was so slight it barely registered.

Axel stepped forward and slugged Rodney in the stomach.

Rodney hunched before falling to his knees. He hadn't expected his cousin to hit him.

"Club before Family," Booster said.

It was the same thing the president had said to him in Moses Lake, but Rodney was sure Booster meant it with the capital 'F' this time.

Axel roughly patted Rodney's body. If he couldn't reach a part of his body, Axel jerked Rodney to a better position, then continued his search. When he was satisfied, Axel muttered, "He's clean."

"Get up," Booster said.

Rodney struggled to catch his breath as he returned to his feet.

"How'd you get free?"

"I escaped," Rodney said weakly. It was another stupid lie, but the truth wouldn't help him now. Rodney was sure of that.

Booster's eyes narrowed. "You escaped? From a Saxon beating and getting shot? Looks like someone tore out some of your hair."

Rodney nodded.

"Then bullshit." Booster shook his head. "They let you go."

"No." Rodney pulled his shoulders back and tried to project a look of confidence. "I escaped."

"Uh-huh." Booster eyed Axel, then lifted his chin.

Rodney's eyes widened and he lifted his hands in defense. "Wait!"

Axel stepped forward and feinted toward the right. Rodney fell for it. Axel hit him in the ribs with his left hand.

The ground rose fast, and Rodney slammed into it. He curled into a ball and tucked his elbow into his side.

Booster squatted next to Rodney. A switchblade flicked open next to his face. "Don't lie," the club president said.

"Now's not the time. I'll gut you here and leave you to bleed out."

Overhead, the announcer called the first event—barrel racing.

"We're missing the rodeo because of you," Axel said.

"You hear that?" Booster asked. "We didn't come up here to fuck around with your nonsense." He tapped the flat of the knife's blade against Rodney's forehead. "Why'd they let you go? No lies."

"I'm not lying."

"Yes, you are." The club president now pointed the knife at Rodney's widened eyes. "The truth shall set you free, Rodney McCready." Booster moved the tip so close it touched Rodney's eyelashes. "You told them you're working with the feds, didn't you?"

"What?"

"Because if you told them you were working with us, they'd have killed you."

Rodney's mouth widened, but he couldn't think of anything to say.

Booster smirked. "We know." He pulled the blade away from Rodney. "Why do you think we sent you up here? We'd never send a prospect to do a job like this."

The club president stood and kicked Rodney in the stomach.

***

Rodney lay on the ground for some time.

The Souls and their biker brethren never broke the circle around him. Inside, Booster and Axel watched Rodney like scientists expecting to witness a chemical reaction.

Overhead, the announcer called out another barrel racer's name.

Axel angrily waved his hand. "Goddamn it, we're missing the whole thing."

"He's your cousin," Booster said.

"Don't hold that against me. I told you what I suspected the moment he showed up."

Booster sniffed. "Yeah. I might've miscalled this one."

Rodney pushed himself to his hands and knees.

"Look who's rising from the dead," Booster said.

"If you knew—" That's all Rodney could get out. His world swayed when he got to his feet, and he was afraid of falling again. His face, shoulder, and ribs hurt. The top of his head, too. It felt like he'd been in the worst collision of his life.

"If we knew about you and the feds," Booster said, "why didn't we do something about it?"

Rodney nodded.

"But we did. We kept you away from everything important."

"Why even let me in the house?"

"Better the devil you know." Booster shoved his hands into his pockets. "We kept an eye on you while we figured out who was watching us. That's why we sent you after Saxon with the promise of earning your patch. Took a while to figure out it was the FBI."

Rodney swallowed with some difficulty. "Shit."

"It's not the first time they've eyed us," Booster said.

"ATF, too," Axel added.

The club president spat. "We've learned over the years not to get panicked in these situations. Doing so only makes things worse. That's why we redirected your attention. We figured if you learned anything about Saxon and the Family, maybe the FBI would get distracted. If not, it kept you out of our hair until we could figure out a plan."

Rodney cocked his head. "Why didn't you just kill me?"

Booster opened his palms. "We couldn't do that, now could we? That would bring all sorts of trouble. Local cops would have been on us like white on rice."

"You're going to kill me now." Rodney's eyes flicked to the opened switchblade.

"Who said that?" Booster lifted his chin.

"Wait," Rodney said.

Axel feinted a punch to the face before punching Rodney in the ribs. Once again, Rodney collapsed to the ground.

Booster squatted next to Rodney. He closed the knife. "So Saxon knows about us, too?"

Rodney nodded.

"Did he wonder why I sent you to him?"

"I told him I didn't know."

Booster smiled with cruelty. "That's great. I picked him for that exact reason. We had some bad blood years ago, but nothing's been between us for years. I needed someone with no real connection to the club."

The dry grass tickled Rodney's face, and he wanted to stand. He didn't like lying there helpless before the club's president.

People walked by the Wasted Souls' protective circle. Some seemed intrigued by what they witnessed, but none were bothered enough to do anything about it.

"We're back to the earlier question," Booster said. "Why did Saxon let you free? He beat you and shot you. He wasn't worried about you running to us and he wasn't worried you running to the FBI. Why?"

"Video," Rodney said.

"What video?"

"Of me killing the guys at the greenhouse."

Booster stood. "That certainly complicates matters."

Rodney struggled to sit upright. His head felt like it might roll off his shoulders. The nausea returned and he swooned. Rodney put a hand on the ground to steady himself. "Saxon is holding a woman. He's going to make it look like I murdered her."

"Unless you do what?"

Rodney stared up at the club president. "I'm supposed to kill you."

Axel eyed Booster. "Guess that bad blood is worse than you remember."

Booster crossed his arms, and his eyes narrowed. "Who's the woman to you?"

"An associate of the Family."

"She's something more," Booster said. "You two hook up?"

Rodney nodded.

Booster's lips pinched as he thought. "The dirty bastard."

Axel motioned toward Rodney. "Him?"

"No," Booster said. "Saxon. He's playing the same game we are. Hot potato." Booster flicked a hand toward Rodney. "Saxon must've figured a couple scenarios could happen by sending this idiot back to us. First, Rodney succeeds."

Axel's eyebrows rose. "And kills you?"

"Stranger things have happened."

"Like what?"

The two men talked about Rodney like he wasn't there. That was fine with him because he struggled to control his nausea. He didn't want to throw up in front of them.

"All sorts of leaders have been assassinated," Booster said. "Presidents. Martin Luther King Jr."

Axel grunted his reluctant acceptance of the club president's argument.

Booster continued. "Hell, that one crazy even got John Lennon."

"The Beatle?"

"You didn't just ask that." Booster smirked. "My point is ol' Rodney the Rat here might have slipped under our radar and succeeded."

Axel shrugged. "The Family doesn't have anything against us."

"No, but it does have a grudge against your cousin and the FBI." Booster smiled. "If he killed me, that's another murder he's carrying. Then we, the Souls, would be after him. Maybe the cops, too, if that killing went down here."

"Wouldn't they charge Saxon and the Family with conspiracy?" Axel asked. "For sending Rodney after you?"

Booster smirked. "The FBI would have to prove their involvement. In this story, I'd be dead, so Saxon would have won regardless of the outcome."

Rodney shook his head. "I wasn't going to do it. That's why I called."

"Maybe to set me up," Booster said.

"I don't have a gun."

Booster's eyes narrowed. "How'd they expect you to kill me?"

Rodney sighed. "Saxon said to get creative."

"There it is." Booster waggled a finger in Rodney's face. "That's where Saxon wants us to do our own dirty work. He's got the video of you murdering those two men, right? He owns your ass now. If you don't follow through and kill me, he turns that video over to the cops. They come for you and the FBI squeezes you. We already know you're a bitch because you ratted once. You'll squeal again."

"I won't talk," Rodney said. "I promise."

Booster pointed at him. "Don't lie."

The club president was correct. Rodney was lying.

"How'd you know I was jammed up?" Rodney asked.

Booster motioned toward Axel. "It was him. Your cousin knew from the moment you showed up."

Axel's eyes darkened. "You had plenty of opportunity to join. You only showed up after you got busted for the bank robbery. It didn't take a genius to figure that out."

Booster hawked a loogie and spat it on the ground near Rodney. "The question is what to do with you now?"

"You can let me go." Rodney stood slowly. "I don't know anything."

"That sounds like a horrible deal," Booster said. "Not only do we look like a bunch of pussies, but what do we get out of it?"

"I've got a plan."

Booster and Axel exchanged glances.

"Hear me out," Rodney said.

17

Choose the Hero

The crowd cheered as the angry bull erupted from the gate. The rider held on as the animal bucked and thrashed. The beast spun, its hind legs kicking wildly. The cowboy's left hand flailed in the air until he was thrown from the bull's back—a rag doll flung to the dirt.

Overhead, the announcer exulted the rider's efforts, and the crowd applauded in response.

A clown jumped over the fence and raced in front of the seething bull as others hurried to the cowboy's aid.

Rodney quit watching then and turned his attention to the stands above him. Had he expected Agent Walker to wave, Rodney would have been disappointed. Appearances must be maintained.

After the roughing up by Booster, Rodney texted Walker for a meeting. The FBI man said he was in the stadium and added a section. Rodney ascended the stairs, scanning the crowd as he went.

The announcer chattered about the next bull rider. When he announced the Suicide Race was less than an hour away, the crowd roared, and the stadium vibrated from stomping feet. Rodney had never been to the Omak Stampede before, let alone a rodeo. He had no idea if crowds found regular events this thrilling.

"Hey," someone shouted. Rodney focused on the voice.

Agent Shane Walker leaned forward from the middle of a nearby row and saluted him with a hot dog.

Neither seat was open next to the FBI agent. Walker said something to the man sitting on his right. The guy stood, glanced at Rodney, and shimmied out of the row in the opposite direction.

"Excuse me," Rodney said to the person sitting closest to him as he squeezed by.

He wriggled by the others in the row until he arrived at the empty seat. Rodney dropped next to the lawman.

Walker appraised him as he finished the final bite of his hot dog. "Jesus, you look like shit," the agent said through a mouthful of food.

"I'm getting that a lot tonight."

"You all right?"

"Been better."

"What's happened?" Walker asked.

"Saxon knows."

A buzzer sounded and another bull burst through the gate. A rider clung to its back as it spun and kicked. Walker didn't care about the scene occurring on the stadium floor. Instead, he studied Rodney.

"He knows what?" the FBI man asked. "That you're working with the Souls?"

Rodney slowly nodded, his attention on the arena. "He also knows I'm working for you."

The bull bucked and threw the cowboy away from its back.

Walker's jaw dropped. "How the hell does he know that?"

"He bugged my apartment, remember?"

The lawman slumped in his chair and faced forward. "Shit."

The rodeo clown was back, doing his best to lure the bull away from the downed cowboy.

"He heard me talking to you," Rodney said. He waved a hand in front of his face and shoulder. "He tortured me until I told the truth."

A woman sitting next to Walker leaned forward now and studied Rodney. She had short blond hair and gray eyes. Her pressed plaid shirt and bright blue jeans suggested she was a tourist.

"Rodney," Walker said, "this is Agent Boothe. Boothe, meet Rodney McCready. Agent Horlander gave up his seat for you."

Rodney nodded.

The woman's eyes shifted to Walker. "The locals could go after the Family for assault. It pulls them off the board and gets McCready back in Spokane."

"The prize is the Souls," Walker said. "The Family is a bonus." He cast a sideways glance. "They sent Rodney up here to get accepted into the Family's inner circle. It's a prospect challenge."

Rodney knew the FBI agent had it wrong, but he didn't dispute the lawman's assertion.

The announcer called the name of the next contestant, a celebrity rider from Dillon, Montana. The crowd politely clapped.

The Fed twisted in his seat. "If you can't get patched in, you're of no help to the U.S. Government."

"I can still get patched in," Rodney lied.

"How's that?"

Before Rodney could lay out his plan, Walker held up a hand.

"Hold on," the agent said. He motioned at Rodney's face and the blood on his shirt. "If Saxon and the Family did that to you, how'd you get away?"

Rodney licked his chapped lips. The agent gave him the

perfect opportunity to tell the lie. He knew he wasn't going to get away with saying he escaped. That story had already failed with the Wasted Souls. Rodney's story had to be better this time. He had to sink the hook so deep, Walker wouldn't dare walk away. Rodney's life and freedom depended on it.

The buzzer sounded and the next bull shot out of the gate. Before Rodney could speak, the crowd gasped. The beast bucked violently and threw the celebrity rider from its back. The cowboy landed awkwardly and didn't move.

A hush fell over the stadium as the clown raced toward the still thrashing bull. Medical personnel sprinted for the fallen rider.

Walker continued to stare at Rodney. "Well?"

He turned back to the lawman. "I made a deal."

"What kind?"

Rodney looked around to make sure no one was listening. Now that the arena had gone quiet to watch the drama surrounding the injured rider, it felt like everyone could hear him. "I'm supposed to kill you," Rodney whispered.

Walker didn't seem phased by the admission. The female agent sitting next to him, however, was completely surprised.

Boothe bolted upright and glanced around once before looking toward the top of the grandstands. Rodney's eyes followed hers. Agent Horlander, the man who'd gotten up a few minutes earlier, watched the three of them. He noticed their sudden change in demeanor and moved toward the stairs. Horlander was going to hem Rodney into this row. There was no escaping this moment.

Rodney looked at Walker again. "It was either kill you," Rodney whispered, "or they'd kill me."

Agent Walker scratched his chin. "You got a gun? A knife?" He waved a hand. "You planning to do it here? In front of all these people?"

"I don't have anything."

Boothe leaned near Walker's ear. "This reeks."

Walker continued. "You going to kill me with your bare hands, Rodney? Like you're Arnold Schwarzenegger or something?"

"I'm supposed to improvise."

"I don't get it." Walker frowned. "Why would they trust you to carry this out? You could run at the first chance of freedom."

"Because they'll kill the woman I like." Lies were always best when the truth was wrapped around them.

"Is that this Electric Mary you told me about?"

Rodney nodded.

"Does she know about this deal?"

"She was there," Rodney said. "They're holding her hostage at the Farm. They'll make it look like I murdered her if I don't kill you. They put my fingerprints on a gun. They made her scratch me so it would look like I attacked her."

Rodney pulled up his T-shirt to show the claw marks Mary had made. Walker grimaced but Boothe eyed them with suspicion.

"They also made her pull out a clump of my hair." Rodney dipped his head.

"I don't like it," Boothe said. She flicked her hand at Rodney. "Maybe he already killed her and is using this as a ruse to put the blame on the Family."

"She's alive," Rodney said. He stared into Walker's eyes. "You know me. I've never killed anyone." Rodney had never tried so hard to convince anyone he was telling the truth.

Walker's eyes narrowed and he scratched the side of his face. "Rodney's not a killer. She's alive."

"What do you want to do?" Boothe asked. "Call HRT?"

"What's that?" Rodney asked.

"Hostage Rescue Team," Walker said. He cocked his head toward the female agent. "Make the call, but it'll take a couple of hours for them to get here."

Boothe pulled a phone from her pocket.

Rodney "Mary might be dead by then."

"We'll also alert local SWAT," Walker said.

"You trust the locals?" Rodney asked. "Some of them might be in Saxon's pocket. He'll know what's headed his way."

Walker's face pinched. "You never said he had ties to the local police."

"I never saw it." Rodney shrugged. "Doesn't mean it's not true."

Boothe held the phone to her ear. "On with supervisor," she whispered. "Standing by."

On the rodeo floor, an ambulance crept in from the east end. Medical personnel stabilized the rider's head as they placed him on a hardboard. Many in the crowd rose to their feet to watch the continuing drama.

Rodney and the two agents remained seated, though. Horlander stood at the end of the row, his gaze affixed to Rodney.

"How many are on the Farm?" Walker asked.

"Five," Rodney said. "Saxon, Wiley, Tucker, Kaylee, and Mary. Nolan's in jail, according to you."

Walker glanced at the female agent. "You get that?"

Boothe nodded. "Still holding for the supervisor."

"With me," Walker said, "there are three agents. What

if we go get your girl back?"

That's what Rodney had hoped he would say. He forced a polite smile. "Thank you."

"On the way to the Farm, you can tell me how you think you can still get patched in." Walker stood. "Let's go."

***

The announcer continued to call events as Rodney and the FBI agents walked out of the arena.

"Coming up next, ladies and gents, steer wrestling." The announcer must have sensed a lull in the crowd's enthusiasm because he quickly added, "Who's excited about the Suicide Race?"

A roar erupted from the stadium.

Nearby a woman entering the arena screamed and waved her beer in the air. "Fucking A, right! Let's go!"

Rodney turned to look and made eye contact with Dancing Arrow.

She smiled and pointed at Rodney. "It's you!"

Her eyes swept over the three FBI agents with him. Even though they were dressed in plain clothes, Dancing Arrow knew something was wrong. Her face hardened. "Nope. I was wrong. Never mind."

Dancing Arrow continued into the stadium.

"Friend of yours?" Agent Walker asked.

"Never saw her before," Rodney said.

He turned his attention forward.

Walker stayed at Rodney's side as they made their way through the crowd.

"How do we know he's telling the truth?" Agent Boothe asked.

"I am," Rodney said. "They're holding Mary hostage."

"Let's run out and recon the house," Horlander said. He was a big man. Two of his strides equaled three of the others.

"We will," Walker said. "We're gonna take it nice and easy, though."

"Is there enough time for that?" Rodney asked.

Walker grunted. "Stop pushing so hard."

"See?" the female agent said. "Feels hinky, right?"

"I've thought about that." Walker stopped, forcing everyone else to halt.

Rodney faced him. "I'm telling the truth."

Walker's face hardened. "Just so you're clear. We're calling this in before we go out to the Farm. Our supervisor will know what's going on. The locals, too. We'll call them at the last minute so the wrong people can't get word to Saxon, but plenty of people will know. Understand? We're not about to pull any cowboy shit."

Just then, a group of men in cowboy hats and western gear walked by.

Horlander and Boothe exchanged glances.

Walker poked Rodney in the chest. "If you think you're setting us up, you've got another thing coming."

Rodney lifted his hands in surrender. "I'm not setting you up."

The lawman swatted Rodney's arms. "Put your hands down." Walker glanced around. "Now that we got that straight." He started walking. The other agents fell in behind him. "Tell me how you think you can still get patched in."

"That's easy," Rodney said. "All you gotta do is arrest me."

Walker stopped walking again. "Say what now?"

The announcer overhead called the first contestant in

the steer wrestling competition. A polite cheer followed. Some '80s rock and roll music drifted from the nearby vendors.

Rodney smiled. "We go out to the Farm, right? We rescue Mary, then you arrest everybody including me."

Walker glanced at Horlander and Boothe before returning to Rodney. "They know about you working with us. You just said."

"Keep the Family away from everyone else," Rodney said. "Put them in solitary or something."

Walker's face pinched. "Do you ever think about what you say?"

"Listen," Rodney said. "If you arrest everyone—"

"I get what you want us to do," Walker said, "but it's not going to work."

Horlander and Boothe pulled in tighter. The three agents stared at Rodney. It made him more uncomfortable than when the Family and the Souls questioned him earlier.

Rodney swallowed. "If you pull the Family off the Farm, the Souls will think it's theirs for the taking."

"No, they won't." Walker glanced at Horlander. The bigger agent shook his head. When Walker glanced at Boothe, she also gestured no. "See? They don't believe your bullshit either. You're pressing again."

"Okay." Rodney said. "Listen—"

Walker held up a finger to interrupt him.

"You know when a shit bag is lying?" Boothe asked.

Rodney stared at her.

"He's talking," the female agent said.

Walker pointed at Rodney. "The only true thing you said tonight is you're supposed to kill me."

"Us." Horlander said.

"Yeah," Boothe added. "Us."

Walker waggled his finger between the other agents.

"They're holding Mary," Rodney said. He clasped his hands together. "I swear to God."

"Nice touch." Walker crossed his arms. "A bit dramatic, don't you think?"

"I don't believe it," Boothe said.

Horlander thumbed over his shoulder. "Does this mean we can still see the Suicide Race?"

Rodney looked toward the starless night sky. "I'm telling the truth."

"Here's what we're willing to do," Walker said. "We'll take you into custody right now."

"What?" Rodney's eyes widened.

"Shit," Boothe said.

"There goes the race," Horlander muttered.

Walker glared at the other male agent.

"What?" Horlander said. "I really wanted to see that race."

Rodney punched one hand into the other. "They're gonna kill Mary!"

Several attendees slowed to watch the interaction between Rodney and the federal agents.

"Make a spectacle, Rodney," Walker said, "but it won't help anything. I've changed my mind. We're not going out to the Farm."

Horlander turned back toward the stadium. "Seriously. Do you care if I go back and watch?"

Walker put his hand on the bigger agent's shoulder. "Hold on."

"What am I supposed to do?" Rodney asked. "Mary needs help."

"Alert the locals."

"But—"

"But nothing," Walker said. "Your cover's blown, and it's no longer safe around here. Anyone can be tied in with the Family. Come with us and we'll keep an eye on you."

Rodney shoulders slumped. "My deal—"

"That's gone," Walker said. "You didn't hold up your end of the bargain so you're going back inside."

"Aw. So sad." Boothe waved at Rodney. "Maybe they kept your cell ready."

Walker patted Horlander's shoulder. "Find us some seats."

The big agent headed toward the arena.

Boothe cocked her head, clearly confused.

"Here's how things are going to play out," Walker said. "We're going back inside to watch the race."

"We are?" Boothe interrupted.

Walker eyed her. "That's why we hung around here."

"We should hook him now." As an afterthought she, added, "Protocol."

"I think Rodney's properly motivated now." Walker turned to him. "Aren't you?"

Rodney frowned. "I don't understand."

"Come Monday morning," Walker said, "I'm revoking your deal."

"Monday?" Boothe asked.

Walker's eyes narrowed as he studied Rodney. "Unless something changes my mind."

A little more than a day, Rodney thought. If he could rescue Mary and recover the CDs, he could get a one-day head start on the U.S. Government. He was near the Canadian border, but that country extradited. However, if he and Mary could get across, maybe they could work their way to another country—assuming she'd want to come with him.

Walker leaned forward and got in Rodney's face. "Don't even think about running north. The border guards will be watching for you."

Rodney couldn't tell if the FBI man was bluffing.

"This isn't right," Boothe muttered.

Walker tapped his watch. "Clock's ticking, convict. What're you going to do?"

Boothe pointed at Rodney. "Don't be a hero. Let's call the locals. We'll take you in now."

No one had ever accused Rodney of being a hero, but for a moment he liked the idea of rescuing Mary. If she was willing to be his perfect girl before, what would she do when he saved her from Saxon?

"I'll handle it," Rodney said as he backpedaled. "You won't do anything until Monday. I've got your word."

Boothe's lip curled. "Not sure that means anything."

Walker glared at her. "Monday," he said. "He's got until Monday."

Rodney almost stopped to ask if the agent had the authority to make a deal like this but thought better of it. Time was wasting, and cops didn't always follow the law. He had to take Walker at his word. There was no other choice.

He spun and trotted toward his car. His shoulder and head hurt with every step.

***

Rodney climbed into his truck. He put his hands on the steering wheel and stared straight ahead. He'd failed. His plan to lure Agent Walker into a clash with the Family was now a pipe dream.

The announcer sounded muffled through the truck's

closed cab. Rodney pressed his head against the steering wheel. What could he do now?

Race back to the Farm and make a daring entrance? With what? He didn't have a gun anymore.

Maybe he could sneak onto the Farm, rummage through the barn, and find a weapon. Rodney sighed. He knew exactly what was in there. He had pulled everything out. There weren't any weapons. Well, nothing he could use to overpower four members of the Family.

Would Kaylee fight him? Maybe not, but she could pull a trigger just as easily as anyone else. Rodney believed she would, too. Especially if it meant her freedom versus his. How could Rodney convince her that he meant no harm?

By going unarmed.

Rodney looked up as a crazy idea took hold. He slowly nodded as the thought became more believable. He'd seen it done in the movies before. The hero, out of bullets or without a gun, often talked an agitated bad guy into giving up his hostage. At least, he thought he saw it in a movie.

Why couldn't Rodney do that? It was his only option.

He closed his eyes. It wasn't his only option. He could split town right now. Run north and be in Canada in an hour. Or run south and be anywhere else. He wasn't sure Mary would go with him anyway. Hell, there were times over the past couple of days he wondered if he even cared about her.

So what changed?

It wasn't hard to figure out. The more his life and freedom hung in the balance, the more Rodney wanted the relationship with Mary to mean something. Especially in a world where nothing else did.

He gripped the steering wheel. If Rodney was a praying man, now would be the time to do such a thing. He'd attended church services several times while in prison. More out of boredom than curiosity. Some of the inmates bought into that mumbo-jumbo. Not Rodney, though. He wasn't raised with faith. He was brought up with the belief it was every man for himself. It's no wonder his mother took off to Arizona so quickly after his father died.

Rodney jumped when someone knocked on the driver's window. He opened his eyes and leaned into the middle of the truck.

Axel stood there, watching Rodney with eyes calloused to the truth. He spun his hand in a circular motion.

Rodney sat upright and he rolled down the window.

"We saw you coming out of the stadium," Axel said. He thumbed over his shoulder. Standing nearby, watching their interaction, was Booster and a contingent of the Wasted Souls. "Who was that with you? The feds?" Hatred flared in Axel's eyes. "It was, wasn't it? I oughta bust you in the mouth."

Rodney glanced around to see if anyone else was watching. Standing between two large trucks was Dancing Arrow. She held a hand near her face as if she were talking to someone on a cell phone. She noticed Rodney watching her and she backpedaled.

"Well?" Axel asked.

"You already hit me," Rodney muttered. "Once more won't make much difference."

Axel reached through the window, snatched Rodney by the shirt and tugged. Rodney grabbed the steering wheel to stop from being yanked out of the truck. The shirt rose around Rodney's throat.

During the struggle, Rodney lost sight of Dancing Arrow. She vanished behind one of the large pickups.

"You should watch that mouth." Axel's fist cocked near

his ear. "It's gonna get you in more trouble than you already are."

"Sorry," Rodney croaked. He really didn't want to be hit again. He also didn't want the other Souls getting involved. Rodney let go of the steering wheel and lifted his hands in surrender. "Really."

Axel let go of the T-shirt, but shoved Rodney in the chest. "Why'd the feds go back inside?"

"I guess they're fans of the rodeo."

Rodney should have expected the punch. Axel had given him plenty of warning. It wasn't an exceptionally hard strike because the two men were so close together and Axel didn't have room to get much force behind it. However, Mary headbutted Rodney earlier and Wiley hit him in the face. Axel's earlier mugging damaged his ribs. Rodney's whole body hurt.

So, Axel's punch across the jaw was enough to feel like a baseball bat had hit Rodney. Rodney collapsed onto the bench seat.

Axel jerked open the driver's door, grabbed Rodney with both hands, and yanked him out of the pickup. The Souls didn't come running, but they scattered about the area, looking to intercept any potential witnesses.

Rodney threw a half-ass punch, but Axel expertly tucked his chin, like a prizefighter squaring off against an untrained opponent. Rodney's fist careened off the crown of Axel's head. It felt like hitting a bowling ball.

Axel swung Rodney around and shoved him backward into the side of the truck. "Answer me," he said, his voice heated with anger.

Rodney couldn't think straight to remember the question Axel had asked only moments before.

He never saw the punch Axel threw into his stomach.

Rodney dropped to his knees and heaved. Nothing came out and his lungs wouldn't take air. His body felt stuck in a panicked loop, unsure of what to do next.

Axel put his hand on the back of Rodney's neck. "Take it easy. Just breath."

Rodney grasped the dirt ground, desperately clinging to the Earth. He opened his mouth, a fish out of water.

The other Souls paid no attention to the two men. They kept scanning for potential witnesses who might need to be discouraged from walking in their direction.

Rodney searched the area for Dancing Arrow but couldn't find her.

"Relax," Axel cooed. It was a strange sound to come from the man. "Just relax." He patted his cousin's neck. "You're gonna be all right."

When air finally reached Rodney's lungs, he sucked deeply. Tears filled his eyes.

Axel stepped away and crossed his arms. He watched his cousin the way a boy might study a fly after ripping its wings off. "Better now?"

Rodney nodded, his head jerking amid ragged breaths.

"Back to my question," Axel said. "Why'd those feds go back inside?"

"They wouldn't help me." Rodney's voice sounded raspy and shaky, a combination he didn't like to hear in his ears. He inhaled deeply to steady himself.

"You told them about the girl?"

Rodney looked up and noticed Booster watching him. The other Souls continued to look for possible witnesses.

"You told them about the girl?" Axel repeated.

"Yeah," Rodney said.

"What'd they say to that?"

"To call the cops."

Axel glanced at Booster. The two men shared a knowing smile.

From the stadium, the announcer said, *"Ladies and gentlemen, we're only ten minutes away from the world-famous Suicide Race. Get your peanuts and popcorn and return to your seats. You don't want to miss this."*

"Did you call the cops?" Axel asked.

"No."

"Why not?"

Rodney used the truck to stand. "Who knows if Saxon has someone in the department? If I call, maybe he kills her."

Axel cocked his head. "Have you lost your deal with the feds?"

Rodney thought about lying to Axel. Instead, he nodded.

"What are you going to do?" his cousin asked.

"Go after the girl."

"You got a gun?"

Rodney shook his head.

Axel studied him. "What's your plan?"

"I don't have one."

"Going after Saxon unarmed is committing suicide." Axel waved a hand. "Hell. Even going after the Family armed is gonna be suicide."

"Maybe not." Rodney didn't believe his own words.

"The girl is bait."

"I know." Rodney's shoulders slumped further. "But I'm not leaving her."

"What happens if you save her?"

"I don't know."

Axel smirked. "Sure you do. You go on the run." He reached underneath his shirt and pulled out a Smith &

Wesson automatic. Rodney stepped back and bumped into the truck. "You see, here's the thing. I'm supposed to decide what to do with you."

Booster no longer watched the interaction between Rodney and Axel. Instead, his head swiveled like the other men in the club. The club's president likely realized how deadly the conversation had become.

Rodney's attention returned to Axel's gun. "You don't have to do this."

"But I do. You ratted on us. Any other day, I'd kill you right now."

"We're cousins," Rodney said weakly.

"Club before family." Axel turned the gun as if inspecting it. "We knew you were dirty from the get-go."

"The feds had me."

"We've all been had," Axel said. "At one time or another, someone's had their hand on our nuts. You do your time like a man. That's how we make it through this life. Otherwise, what are we?"

Free, Rodney thought, but he kept it to himself.

Axel tapped the gun barrel against the palm of his opposite hand. "I let you walk away from here doesn't mean we forgive. It just means you serve a purpose. Understand?"

Rodney stared at his cousin.

"Because no matter what you do at the Farm, no matter how bloody it gets—" Axel leaned closer to study Rodney. "The Souls will never forgive what you've done."

"I know."

"It sounds like the feds are gonna be after you, too. If they get you, you're going inside for the bank robbery."

Rodney nodded.

"If you land in any prison, the Souls can get you. We'll

make your life miserable before we end it. That's a promise."

Again, Rodney nodded.

"So, what's it going to be? Want me to end your suffering here and now? Or do you wanna be hero?"

"I'll choose the hero."

Axel used the tail of his T-shirt to wipe down the gun's barrel and grip. "You're gonna need this."

Rodney accepted it. His eyes cut to Booster and the other Souls. Many of them were already heading toward the stadium.

"Why are you helping me do this?" Rodney asked. "The bad blood with Saxon was old. It was settled."

Axel set his hand on Rodney's shoulder and stared his cousin in the eye. "Bad blood is never old. It's never settled. Saxon made a mistake by sending you back."

Rodney was afraid to ask, but it was Axel. He hoped the man remembered their childhood moments together. "Aren't you making the same mistake as Saxon?"

Axel patted Rodney's shoulder. "You're dead no matter what, cousin. I'm giving you a chance to do it with some honor. If you don't want it…"

Rodney held the gun with both hands. "No. I want it."

"I'd wish you good luck, Rodney, but it doesn't matter."

Axel spun on his heel and joined Booster. The Wasted Souls headed for the stadium.

18

A Method to Any Madness

The August sun lingered over the western horizon as Rodney McCready raced toward the Farm. The speedometer crested seventy-five, fifteen miles per hour over the legal limit. While he drove, Rodney didn't plan how to confront Saxon Peckham and the Family. He also didn't make peace with the God he barely believed in.

Instead, Rodney thought back on his life. He rapidly sifted through the stupid decisions he'd made, the trouble he'd found, and the hurt he'd caused. Sadly, Rodney couldn't find one heroic moment. There wasn't a single, selfless act where he came to the aid of another.

Then why was he barreling eastbound on WA-155 toward a group who wished him either dead or back in prison?

Was it for love? Was it really because Mary claimed she'd be his perfect girl?

Rodney used the steering wheel to pull himself higher in his seat. He ignored the road as he studied the rearview mirror. "Dumb ass," he said to his reflection. Rodney dropped back into place.

An emotion rolled over him. At first, Rodney thought it was remorse, but he quickly decided it was disappointment. He wanted his actions to be for love. Rodney had watched plenty of movies in his life where the hero saved the girl. Dramatic music often rose to accompany scenes of smiles and kisses.

Rodney smacked his palm against the steering wheel.

Maybe if Mary really loved him, he could pull off heroic deeds for her. How could he be sure? Rodney shook his head. He needed to clear those thoughts away. He could never trust anyone to tell the truth about any situation, let alone himself.

Rodney's politician father had often blathered about honesty. That it had healing powers and it could redeem a hurting soul. Rodney knew it was bullshit, especially since his father lied more than Rodney ever could. His father was even aware of his wife's multi-year affair, but they both pretended nothing was wrong. If Rodney's parents treated honesty with such disrespect, then how could he handle the truth any better?

"Focus!" Rodney gripped the steering wheel and angrily shook himself.

The truck swerved. Rodney stopped his antics and paid attention to the road.

The only reason to return to the Farm was to recover the evidence, both actual and contrived. Rodney needed to grab the CDs containing the video footage from the greenhouse. Then Rodney would destroy the bag of evidence the Family put together for Mary's yet-committed murder.

What Rodney didn't want to consider were the acts he might need to commit to recover those items. Until the greenhouse incident, he never killed anyone. With the life he'd led and the choices he'd made, Rodney had been lucky to avoid that.

Tonight he might be forced to do it again.

Saxon and the Family surely wouldn't allow him to take the discs. The Savage Renegades demanded someone be held responsible for the greenhouse robbery. Rodney didn't know what Tucker had told them to get a copy of the video. Perhaps the Family promised their help. Or maybe the attorney for the Renegades already viewed the video and made the connection. The man saw Rodney pulling debris from the barn several days ago. He could link the Family to the incident. Saxon had to make Rodney responsible.

Now, Rodney saw the truth in Saxon's earlier deal.

Even if Rodney had killed Booster, there was no way the Old Man would have honored their deal. Saxon needed to save face with the Renegades. He would confirm the Family's link to Rodney with the west side biker club. In an act of good faith, Saxon would also return the money Rodney stole. Retribution had to be made. Rodney didn't want to think about what lay after.

He pulled his truck to the side of the highway and stopped. The Farm was a quarter mile ahead. If Rodney wanted to sneak up on them, he'd have to wait for nightfall. An hour or more, at least.

Saxon's house sat back at least a hundred yards from the road. The long, dusty roadway was narrow and led right to the front. Walking or driving up its path was tantamount to ringing a doorbell.

Rodney could abandon his truck where it was and take a circuitous route by foot through the scrub brush. It would take much longer than he wanted to get to the Farm. Anything could happen to Mary by then.

Would Saxon harm her out of spite? Rodney didn't know. Maybe he'd hurt Mary to show the Family he kept his word. There were too many variables to consider.

Wiley would be there. Perhaps he'd hurt Mary because she rejected him. Then again, he might still have feelings for her and wouldn't participate.

Tucker probably would. His old cellmate was so angry at Rodney that he could hurt Mary to get back at him. Kaylee wouldn't seem eager to participate in something like that.

So, it seemed unlikely they'd hurt Mary for no reason. Saxon would only do so to motivate Rodney. If the Old Man thought he had Rodney under control everything would be fine.

Rodney opened his door and was about to leave the truck when his cell phone rang. He checked its display—Saxon. Rodney answered the call. "Hello?"

"How much longer?" Saxon asked.

Rodney frowned. "Not much." It was a noncommittal statement. He could switch directions in plenty of ways once he knew Saxon's intent for calling.

"A little birdie said you left the Stampede."

Dancing Arrow, Rodney thought. "She's wrong," Rodney lied.

"So you're still there?"

"That's right."

Further down the highway, a semi headed in Rodney's direction. Sunlight glinted off its windshield. Rodney climbed back into pickup and gently pulled the door closed after him.

"How was the Suicide Race?" Saxon asked.

Rodney leaned into the middle of the cab and covered the cell phone with his free hand. The semi roared by.

"The race was good," Rodney said.

"First time you've seen it?" The Old Man's voice softened.

"Yeah."

"It's something, huh?"

"Yeah."

"You fucking liar." Saxon's tone sharpened. "The race was delayed."

Rodney sat upright. He remained quiet.

The Old Man continued. "Some protesters blocked the river, spouting their animal cruelty bullshit. You would have known if you hung around."

Rodney rested his head on the steering wheel.

"I've got eyes everywhere," Saxon said. "You know this."

"I saw Dancing Arrow."

"She saw the Wasted Souls. She said you were getting pretty chummy with one of them."

Rodney scoffed. "He kicked my ass."

"Something finally rings true. Arrow says you left the Stampede."

"I haven't left," Rodney lied again.

"You knew what failure meant."

Rodney stared down the highway. "You were going to kill her either way."

"I have no idea what you're talking about."

The phone call ended.

Rodney dropped the truck into Drive and stomped the accelerator. The truck fishtailed along the shoulder of the highway. He checked the rearview mirror before entering the appropriate lane.

There was no need for subtlety now.

Saxon knew Rodney hadn't killed Booster. The Old Man had to figure the Wasted Souls now knew about the assignment Saxon had given Rodney. They'd want revenge on the Family one way or another. Saxon was about to be stuck between two biker clubs. He might even wonder if Rodney talked with the feds.

Saxon's first course of action would be to make nice

with one of them. It would be easy to call the Savage Renegades and inform them about Rodney's involvement in the greenhouse incident.

He had only one course of action now—get to the Farm as fast as possible. He'd save Mary if he could, but she was his secondary mission. His primary focus was to locate the CDs and the bag of contrived evidence.

No one ever accused Rodney McCready of being a hero. He wasn't going to prove them wrong tonight.

* * *

The pickup swayed as Rodney drove slowly up the dusty driveway. His gaze swept over the compound, looking for any movement. The hanging flags in the windows—the American, the Confederate, and the Gadsden—remained still.

Three trucks belonging to Wiley, Tucker, and Kaylee were parked in front of the house. Saxon's rarely left the garage.

Rodney stopped his pickup and climbed out. He grabbed his phone and took a moment to dial a number. He checked that it was ringing and slipped it into the front pocket of his pants. Rodney carried Axel's gun in his right hand as he crept toward the house and entered as quietly as he could. The curtains were drawn, but the evening's fading sunlight crept around their edges. Rodney's shadow extended across the kitchen floor.

He stepped out of the doorway and the shadow vanished into the darkened recesses. Rodney closed the door and listened to the home's silence. The quiet unsettled Rodney since the television was usually on while the Family conversed loudly over its programming.

"Back here," Kaylee called.

Rodney stiffened when he heard her voice. He lifted his gun higher and pointed it toward the dining room. Rodney waited for her to say something further, but she remained quiet.

A semi roared down the highway. When its engine faded into the distance, Rodney cautiously left the kitchen. He expected someone to step out of the hallway or the dining room and confront him. He'd be forced to make a choice then—kill or die.

Rodney peeked around the corner, trying to get a better look into the living room, but he couldn't see Kaylee. He stepped into the room, hugging the walls as much as he could. Rodney kept the gun at eye level, prepared to shoot.

He moved to the edge of the entryway. Rodney brought the gun up to the side of his head in a preparatory hold. He'd never been taught to do this. Action stars always did this in the movies before they entered a new room. It seemed the right stance to take.

"I hear you," Kaylee said. She sounded calm.

Rodney peeked around the corner and immediately pulled back.

Before he could comprehend what he saw, Kaylee said, "I'm alone."

He peeked again.

Kaylee sat cross-legged on the couch. A lamp on the end table illuminated the room in a hazy yellow glow. Underneath it sat the three CDs. On the floor was the paper bag.

She inhaled on a cigarette, then turned her head to exhale a plume of smoke. "I'm unarmed."

Rodney stepped around the corner. He held the automatic at eye level. "Stand up," Rodney whispered.

"I don't have any—"

"Now."

Kaylee brought her legs out from underneath her and stood. She lifted her hands in the air. "Why would I lie?"

"Everybody lies." Rodney flicked his wrist which spun the barrel of the gun. "Turn around."

She extended her arms and slowly whirled. No gun was hidden in the back of her denim shorts. "Satisfied?"

Rodney snapped his wrist twice and the gun barrel jerked left and right. "Flip the cushions."

Kaylee frowned. "If I wanted to shoot you—"

He snapped his wrist twice more.

"Whatever."

Kaylee flipped up the cushions. Nothing was hidden underneath them.

"Sit down," he said.

She slapped the cushions into place before dropping onto the middle one. Kaylee brought her legs underneath her. She sucked defiantly on the cigarette.

"Where is everyone?" Rodney asked.

Kaylee turned her head and blew out the smoke. "In the barn. Waiting for you."

"Why aren't you out there?"

She looked down. "That's not my scene."

"Which is what—my death?"

Her eyes burned. "You're working with the feds. How you die doesn't matter to me."

"Then what is it?"

Kaylee rolled the cigarette between her fingers.

"Mary," Rodney said. He'd been right. Kaylee wouldn't take part in her murder.

She concentrated on her hands. "They're waiting for you."

Rodney stepped around Saxon's recliner and grabbed the CDs. If he rescued Mary, the bag of phony evidence wouldn't mean anything. If he died trying, it meant the same. He started to leave the room but stopped. "Why did they leave these in here?"

Kaylee cocked her head. "Huh?"

He waved the discs at the bag of phony evidence. "Why did they leave these unprotected?"

She shrugged. "Because they knew you'd come for the girl."

Rodney felt a rush of excitement. He could grab the bag of evidence and run.

Kaylee put the cigarette in her mouth but didn't inhale. "That's why you came back, isn't it?"

"Yeah," Rodney said automatically. The word sounded hollow by itself, so he added, "Of course." He studied Kaylee. "I thought you hated Mary."

"She's part of the Family." Kaylee inhaled on the cigarette now.

"Wiley called her an associate."

"He would." Kaylee rolled her eyes. "Mary always did what Saxon asked, even when it went against her best interests. The Old Man took care of her mother like she was his sister. What's that sound like to you?"

"Family."

Kaylee pointed at the barn. "He'll sacrifice her if you don't play ball." She tapped her stomach. "That's what makes me sick."

Rodney stiffened. "I'll get her safe."

"There's only one way for you do that," Kaylee said.

"How's that?"

"Shoot yourself in the head."

Rodney stepped back. There was no way he'd do that.

Kaylee shrugged. "Like I said, it's not my scene."

***

Rodney stopped in the kitchen and broke the three CDs. First in half. Then once again. He cut his hand twice doing it, but it was a small price to pay. He gathered up the broken pieces and stepped outside as quietly as he could.

The sun dipped beyond the horizon, casting a hue of purples and oranges across the evening sky. The romantics believed sunsets like this were meant for lovers and forever promises. Rodney knew too well dusk held hurt and disappointment. He'd watched too many sunsets through the narrow window of his Coyote Ridge prison cell.

Rodney flicked the broken CD chunks about the Farm. The jagged portions glimmered in the dying sunlight like fireflies. It took only a moment to scatter them.

Darkness would soon overtake the Farm, yet it wouldn't come fast enough to help Rodney. He hunched and hurried across the driveway. His footsteps crunched on the gravel. As he approached the barn, he slowed and eased along its outer wall. Cracks in the boards allowed him to see inside.

Mary sat in one of the old dining room chairs. The second one sat across from her—empty. The men in the Family awaited Rodney's arrival.

She wasn't tied to her chair like Rodney had been yesterday. Mary was scared, however. Tucker stood next to her, a gun dangling from his hand.

A small blue duffel bag and a leather briefcase were nearby on the ground.

Saxon walked behind Tucker and Mary with a cell

phone pressed to his ear. He mumbled something, then hung up.

Rodney leaned to get a better look through the crack. He couldn't find Wiley. Where was the man hiding? Spooked at Wiley's absence, Rodney glanced behind him. No one was there.

"He's on his way," Saxon said.

Surely, they'd heard Rodney drive up. Maybe Kaylee called from inside to say he was on his way out.

"We don't need him," Tucker said.

Rodney stiffened slightly. Maybe they were talking about Wiley. Was he not inside the barn with Tucker and the Old Man? Once again, Rodney looked around the Farm but didn't see anyone else.

"Shh," Saxon hissed. "Listen."

Rodney froze. His heartbeat pounded inside his ears.

Returning to the Farm had been a bad idea.

The CDs containing the greenhouse video and the bag of phony evidence were only an excuse to pretend to be a hero. Rodney couldn't keep his desires straight in his head. Nothing stopped him from getting in his truck and leaving the Farm right then.

The ramifications for taking a stand were inside the barn. Saxon, Wiley, and Tucker would likely kill him. Maybe Mary would get caught in the crossfire.

What if Rodney took off right then? He could back away from the barn, jump into his truck and hightail it away from the Farm. Maybe the Family would chase him for a time, but for how long? Eventually, they'd give up, right?

That wouldn't be the end of it, Rodney knew.

The Family could probably still get another copy of the greenhouse incident from the Savage Renegades. Saxon would carry through on his threat of delivering the video to the cops. Rodney would be wanted for those two murders.

The Savage Renegades and the Wasted Souls would chase after Rodney for different, more permanent reasons.

To top it off, if Rodney made it to Monday, Agent Walker would cancel his informant deal. The FBI would force Rodney to serve time for the robbery he committed. All the risks he'd taken with the Wasted Souls and the Family meant nothing.

Saxon would never have to kill Mary. It would serve no purpose.

A car raced down the highway. Its little engine sounded horrible because of a missing muffler, like a lawnmower long past its prime. With the added noise, Rodney quickly decided on a course of action—leave now. He'd make a run for the Canadian border and deal with the repercussions tomorrow.

Rodney stepped backward, further away from the barn's opening. Something hard pressed into his lower back.

"Drop the gun," Wiley said, "or I'll shoot you in the back."

Rodney opened his hand and the gun he held rolled backward. It dangled on his finger by the trigger guard.

Wiley shoved his firearm harder into Rodney's spine. "Do it."

Rodney turned his hand and the gun dropped to the ground.

Saxon stepped out of the barn. "It's nice of you to finally arrive." With a ringmaster's flourish, he motioned Rodney inside. "We've saved a spot for you."

 ∗∗∗

Wiley delighted in tying Rodney to the second dining chair. He chattered the entire time he secured Rodney's wrists and ankles to the chair. As he finished the final knot, he said, "I'm getting good at this."

"A regular boy scout," Rodney said. "You should get a merit badge."

Wiley straightened. "Something's not right."

Rodney eyed him.

"What do you think?" Wiley asked Mary.

She stared directly at Rodney. "I'm sorry."

"Oh, that's right," Wiley said. He punched Rodney in the temple and Mary screamed.

Rodney's chair tilted sideways, and he couldn't stop its momentum.

Mary started to leave her chair. Tucker's hand clamped on her shoulder and held her in place.

The fall seemed to take forever. When the chair finally hit, Rodney's head banged against the ground. A ringing in his ears started and the earlier nausea returned.

Saxon grunted. "Get him up."

Wiley shrugged. "I was just having some fun."

A car rumbled up the driveway.

The Old Man twirled his hand. "He's here."

Wiley grabbed Rodney and hefted him back into place. "Not sure why we can't do this ourselves."

"Because," Saxon said, "there's a method to any madness. This is ours."

Outside the barn, a car door opened and closed. Footsteps approached.

The Old Man pointed at Rodney. "Put some tape over his mouth."

Wiley hurried to a small duffel bag and retrieved a roll of duct tape.

"Saxon," Rodney said, "you don't need to do this."

"Hush yourself," the Old Man said. "Know when it's over."

Rodney couldn't give up yet. "Tucker, please."

Tucker's face hardened. "You brought this on yourself."

Wiley ripped off a piece of duct tape from the roll. He hurried to Rodney and stuck it over his mouth. "That'll shut you up." Wiley playfully slapped the side of Rodney's face before backing away.

"This the man?" a warm, male voice asked.

Rodney turned left and right to see who the new arrival was, but he couldn't see him.

"Yeah," Saxon said. "As promised."

A tall, broad-shouldered man came into view. It was the man Saxon described as the lawyer for the Renegades. He wore a dark, nicely cut suit with a white shirt and red tie. His salt and pepper hair was cut in a businessman's swoop. His attention wasn't on Rodney but rather Mary. The lawyer cupped her chin and turned her face up to him. "Who's this?"

"Electric Mary," Tucker said.

"I wasn't asking you."

Tucker glanced at Saxon and Wiley, but both men watched the lawyer for their cues.

The lawyer stroked Mary's hair with his other hand. "Well?"

She looked up at him like a scared puppy seeking acceptance. "Mariam," she said. "Mariam Coleman."

"Why aren't you tied up, Mariam?"

Mary swallowed with some difficulty as the lawyer

continued to hold her chin. "I didn't do anything wrong."

"Is that so?" The lawyer glanced at Saxon. "Why's she sitting across from the man?"

"They were intimate."

"Intimate, huh?" The lawyer waggled Mary's chin. "Is that true, girl?"

Her eyes widened.

"He has feelings for her," Saxon said.

"What about you, Mariam?" The lawyer tugged Mary's chin up higher, and she winced. "Do you have feelings for this man?"

"No." Her eyes darted to Rodney. "I didn't. I don't."

"Good girl." The lawyer let go of her face. He eyed Tucker. "Tie her up."

Mary blurted, "But I said—"

"You lied."

Tucker held Mary in her chair. "Grab more rope," he said to Wiley.

Wiley stood frozen.

"Is there a problem?" the lawyer asked.

"No," Wiley said woodenly. He slowly moved toward the duffel bag.

Saxon stepped closer to Rodney. "We apologize for this situation and hope this makes it right."

"You have the money?" the lawyer asked.

The Old Man pointed to a briefcase. "The twenty-four thousand is all there. He spent some of it, but we made it right."

"As you should. He was your man, after all."

Saxon shook his head. "He was never part of the Family."

The lawyer squatted before Rodney and studied him. "How'd he get in your organization?"

"He served time with one of the boys."

"Which one?"

"Me," Tucker said.

The lawyer looked back. "You found him trustworthy enough to allow in the Family?"

Tucker's fingers dug into Mary's shoulders. She grimaced. "He was never a part of us," Tucker said.

"Hey," Wiley whispered. He lifted his chin toward Mary. "Ease up."

"Before we kill you," the lawyer said to Rodney, "What've you got to say for yourself?" He grabbed the tape covering Rodney's lips and ripped it away.

Rodney widened his mouth and fought back the desire to shout in anger. When he finally got control of the pain, Rodney said, "You should rethink what you're about to do."

"Ignore him," Saxon said. "He'll say anything to cover his ass."

The lawyer lifted a hand to interrupt the Old Man. "Why?" he asked Rodney. "Because of the Souls? Saxon told us."

"No, because of the FBI."

"The FBI?" The lawyer stiffened. "Who's talking to the FBI?"

"You are."

The lawyer slowly stood. A bemused smile crossed his face. "You're claiming to be an FBI man? After what you did?"

"Check my pocket."

"Wiley," Saxon snapped. "Didn't you frisk him?"

Wiley turned his palms upward. "He didn't have anything 'cept his wallet and phone."

"His phone," the lawyer said. He snapped his fingers

and pointed at Rodney.

"Get it," Saxon hissed.

Wiley stepped around the Old Man and dug into Rodney's pocket. He pulled out the phone and turned it over to see the screen. Wiley's eyes lit up. "He's called someone."

"You're talking with Agent Walker of the FBI," Rodney said.

Wiley extended the phone toward the lawyer who stepped back and flopped onto Mary's lap. She yelped in surprise. The lawyer hopped back to his feet.

"Put it on speaker," Rodney said.

Wiley glanced at the lawyer before facing Saxon. Fear filled his eyes, and he continued to hold the phone at arm's length.

"Do it," the Old Man said.

Wiley brought the phone closer and tapped the speaker button.

"Agent Walker?" Rodney asked loudly.

"I'm here."

The lawyer regained some confidence and pointed at the phone. "That could be anyone. Hang up."

Wiley started to press a button on the phone.

"Do what you want," Agent Walker said, "but let me tell you what I know."

Wiley's finger hovered over the screen. His eyes darted to Saxon and the lawyer.

Agent Walker continued. "Present in the room are Family members Saxon Peckham, Tucker Skillingstad, and Wiley Jones. I don't know where Kaylee Zavala is."

"She's in the main house," Rodney said.

Wiley angrily kicked some dirt at him.

Agent Walker kept talking. "You're holding Rodney

McCready and Mariam Coleman against their wills. Isn't that correct?"

"Yes," Rodney said loudly. "We're tied to chairs and can't leave." He nodded to Mary.

"Yes," she called toward the phone. "Like Rodney said."

"They're planning to kill us," Rodney said.

"Not true," the lawyer said. He shook his head and waved his hands. "That could be anyone on the other end of the line. Hang up."

Wiley's finger hovered over the screen.

"You're right," Walker said. "I could be anyone, but in a couple moments, the first deputies are going to arrive at the Farm. We'll be a couple of minutes behind. Then you'll know I am who I say I am."

The lawyer's face whitened.

"So, my friend, who are you?" Walker asked. "Who is this unaccounted-for voice?"

"He's the lawyer for the Savage Renegades," Rodney said.

The lawyer glared at Rodney.

Agent Walker chuckled. "The Renegades, huh? We're really moving up the food chain. We're going to want to talk with you."

The lawyer jumped forward, grabbed the phone from Wiley, and ended the call. He slammed it into the dirt. "Kill him," he said to Saxon.

"No." The Old Man stepped backward. He motioned to Tucker. "Cut her loose. Cut them both loose."

Tucker stared at Saxon, confused.

"Hurry," the Old Man said. He moved toward Rodney.

Sirens wailed in the distance.

The lawyer faced Wiley. "How much to kill this one?"

He pointed at Rodney.

Wiley kneeled next to Rodney's chair and pulled at the knots covering one ankle. "No way I'm going down for this fuckhead's murder."

Saxon clawed at the ropes around Rodney's hands.

The lawyer moved toward the barn's opening. "If any of you tell them who I am—" He let the threat hang in the air before dashing toward his car.

An engine started. Soon, a vehicle raced from the Farm. Sirens continued approaching.

The ropes loosened around Rodney's hands and his first ankle.

"You can do the other," Wiley said. He moved to help Tucker untie Mary.

Saxon moved toward the barn's opening. "Leave your guns."

"Why?" Tucker asked. He moved around Mary and glared at Rodney. "I'm never going back in."

"You'll do what I say," Saxon said. "We'll survive this. I've seen the way." He eyed Rodney.

"I won't do that." Tucker's face reddened. "Never in a million years."

The Old Man pointed at Tucker. "You'll do what I say. Leave and let's go." He stepped outside.

Rodney scrambled to get the rope free from his ankle. His eyes darted from Tucker to Mary and Wiley.

Tears filled Tucker's eyes as he looked toward the barn's ceiling. Eventually, the gun slipped from his fingers and tumbled to the ground. He shuffled outside.

When Wiley freed Mary from the chair, he stepped back. "I'm sorry."

She hopped to her feet. "Get away from me."

He turned his palms upward, pleading with her. "I

wouldn't have let anything happen to you."

Mary backpedaled. "You would have, and you know it."

Wiley stared at her for a moment before slumping his shoulders. He trudged toward the barn's opening.

Sirens filled the night as patrol cars raced up the Farm's driveway. Brakes locked and the various cars skidded. Doors opened and deputies barked orders.

"On the ground!"

"Face the other way!"

"Hands behind your head!"

Rodney stepped to Mary, but her face pinched.

"No," she said. "Never with a rat."

Melted Butter

Red and blue lights bounced off the various buildings of the Farm. Spotlights from the patrol cars lit up the house and barn. It was like being at an outdoor disco club.

The Family members were handcuffed and separated. Rodney knew why the cops did this. It was to stop the Family from communicating with each other and developing a story. Agent Shane Walker hovered near the deputy interviewing Saxon. Agent Horlander bounced between the three deputies interviewing Tucker, Wiley, and Kaylee.

Mary stood near the garage with her arms crossed. She stole an occasional glance at Rodney while Agent Boothe interviewed her. Anytime Rodney caught her looking, Mary's face hardened.

He knew the truth. She'd never forgive him.

Rodney sat with his back against the barn and watched it all. A deputy had tried to interview him, but Agent Walker shooed him away. Rodney's time for talking would have to wait.

He rested his arms on his knees and enjoyed the chaos around him. Just a few days prior, he'd hauled debris out of the barn to earn his way into the Family. Tonight, he helped bust it up.

The voices were plentiful, and Rodney couldn't make out a single line of questioning. Police radios chirped and dispatchers transmitted information. The whole cacophony was difficult to follow.

Saxon's hands were cuffed behind his back, but he motioned into the house by jerking his head. Walker stiffened and asked another question. The Old Man nodded several times, then jerked his head toward the house again. The FBI man bounded the stairs. He stopped at the door and looked back at Rodney, then he entered the house.

Rodney leaned his head against the barn and stared up into the sky. With all the police lights, he couldn't see any stars. He lowered his gaze and waited for Agent Walker to return.

When he did, the FBI man trotted down the steps and spoke with Saxon. Afterward he approached Agent Horlander and Kaylee. The three chatted for a couple of moments. As they did, Walker bent and picked up something from the dirt. He held it up to the light then cupped it in his fist.

Rodney stood as the FBI ambled over.

"Hell of a night," Walker said.

"I thought you weren't going to help."

"You handed us a kidnapping in progress. We had to help." The agent thumbed over his shoulder. "Saxon's willing to deal. Sounds like Kaylee is, too. The others will require some more effort, but they'll come around."

"What about Mary?"

"She's not in trouble." Walker shrugged. "At least, none we can see tonight."

"That's good."

"One little problem, though."

"What's that?" Rodney asked.

"Saxon said you murdered a couple guys at a Davenport greenhouse. You never said anything about an incident like that."

Rodney rolled down his lower lip. "That's because it never happened. The Old Man is just blowing smoke."

Walker cocked his head. "That so? Kaylee's saying the same thing."

"Don't know what to tell you."

The FBI man pulled his hand from his pocket. In the middle of his palm was a shard from one of the broken CDs. "Both of them said there was video footage of the incident. Three CDs. Saxon and Kaylee were clear about that. Kaylee said you took them. This looks like a piece from one."

Rodney feigned confusion. "Sounds like sour grapes."

"Sour grapes?" Walker smiled. "They said the greenhouse was a money laundering operation for the Savage Renegades."

"No shit?"

"You robbed it at the direction of the Wasted Souls. How'd that happen?"

Rodney shook his head. "They're setting me up. I didn't do what they're saying."

Agent Walker shoved his hands into his pockets. "The problem with you, Rodney. I don't know where the truth ends, and the bullshit starts." He jerked his head in the direction of Saxon. "He's going to work with us against the Renegades. We'll hook him and Kaylee up with our Seattle counterparts and get them into the system."

"What about the Wasted Souls? What about me?"

Walker rolled his eyes. "You, you lucky son of a bitch. You get to be a victim. The Family kidnapped you and were planning to kill you at the request of the Renegades' legal counsel. You play your part and do a good job, we'll keep you out of the system."

Rodney imagined sitting before a judge someday to

testify about what he had experienced on the Farm. A smart defense attorney would certainly call into question Rodney's criminal history and how he avoided serving prison time on a robbery conviction.

Walker leaned in. "However, things will get pulled off the table if we find out you murdered anyone. There's no defense for that. Got it?"

"Yeah, sure." Rodney nodded. "You've got nothing to worry about." The lie slid off his tongue like melted butter.

The FBI man eyed him a moment longer. "I'll be in touch in the next couple of days. We'll make sure your new paperwork is squared away."

"Witness protection?"

Walker shrugged a single shoulder. "If you hold up your end of the bargain, you'll get a fresh start." The FBI man walked away.

Mary stood by herself now. Rodney walked over.

"I'm sorry," he said.

"I'm not buying it." Her expression soured.

"I'd like to start over."

Mary crossed her arms. "Not if you were the last man on earth and the human race was about to die out." She stalked away and didn't look back.

Rodney walked to the barn. He noticed Axel's gun laying in the grass. None of the cops had noticed it yet. He sat several feet away from it. If none of them picked it up before it was time to leave, Rodney would grab it.

He didn't have an immediate need for a gun, but who knew with the way life had gone in the past few days.

Bad luck had a way of following Rodney.

Did You Enjoy the Book?

Thank you for reading *The Wasted Pawn* and visiting the 509! I hope you enjoyed meeting some of the recurring characters. This is a continuing series with other characters occasionally stepping into the lead role. There are two parallel series to the 509 Crime Stories—the Flip-Flop Detective and the John Cutler mysteries. I hope you'll check them out.

I'm always grateful when a reader takes time out of their day to comment on one of my novels. If you do write a review, please email me, and let me know.

I'd love to say thanks!

About the Author

Colin Conway is the creator of the 509 Crime Stories, a series of novels set in Eastern Washington with revolving lead characters. They are standalone tales and can be read in any order.

He also created the Cozy Up series which pushes the envelope of the cozy genre. Libby Klein, author of the Poppy McAllister series, says *Cozy Up to Death* is "Not your grandma's cozy."

Colin co-authored the Charlie-316 series. The first novel in the series, *Charlie-316*, is a political/crime thriller that has been described as "riveting and compulsively readable," "the real deal," and "the ultimate ride-along."

He served in the U.S. Army and later was an officer of the Spokane Police Department. He has owned a laundromat, invested in a bar, and run a karate school. Besides writing crime fiction, he is a commercial real estate broker.

Colin lives with his beautiful girlfriend, three wonderful children, and a codependent Vizsla that rules their world.

Find out more at colinconway.com.